DARK DEMON

BOOK FIVE IN THE ANGEL CHRONICLES SERIES

ESTER LÓPEZ

Writing & Photographic Services LLC

For all the brave men and women who serve their communities by enforcing the law to protect us from harm. For those who believe in a higher power and Divine Intervention, and for all the fans of "Golden Idols," this is for you.

PRAYER OF PROTECTION

St. Michael, the Archangel, defend us in battle. Be our defense against the wickedness and snares of the devil. May God rebuke him, we humbly pray; and do you, Prince of the heavenly host, by the power of God, thrust into hell Satan and all the other evil spirits who prowl about the world for the ruin of souls. Amen.

Most Sacred Heart of Jesus, have mercy on us. (three times)

THE ARMOR OF GOD

Ephesians 6:10-17

Finally, grow strong in the Lord with the strength of his power. Put God's armor on, so as to be able to resist the Devil's tactics. For it is not against human enemies that we have to struggle, but against the Sovereignties and the Powers who originate the darkness in this world, the Spiritual Army of evil in the heavens. That is why you must rely on God's Armor, or you will not have enough resources to hold your ground.

So stand your ground, with truth buckled around your waist, and integrity for a breastplate, wearing for shoes on your feet, the eagerness to spread the gospel of peace, and always carrying the shield of faith so that you can use it to put out the burning arrows of the evil one, and then you must accept salvation from God to be your helmet, and receive the word of God from the Spirit to use as a sword.

1

———

Detective Elena Romero Cummings glanced at her notes, then spoke to Keith from the tech team. "Got anything, Keith?"

She stood in the middle of a small repair shop in downtown Miami. The shop owner called when he came to open for business and discovered he had been robbed.

Keith worked on the register, while Danny worked on the door facing, trying to get fingerprints. Amanda photographed footprints.

"I might have a print we can work with. Whoever did this was good," Keith said.

There hadn't been much damage except at the doorway. It appeared to be ripped open with a crowbar. And the register was not damaged. The guy either worked here or knew something about registers.

Her partner, Pete Cummings, walked up to her. "They didn't have an alarm system and only took money from the register," he said.

"This one is a little tougher, Pete. Keith may have a print, but I'm not getting my hopes up."

"There's something else," he leaned in and whispered.

She glanced up at his tall frame. Pete looked around the small shop, a scowl on his face. "I smell a demon."

"A demon? Like in Satan?"

"Yes. This may have been done by a human, but there was a demon in this store."

"Well, that's a first. I've never hunted a demon before."

"I pray we never have to, Elena."

She got the owner's phone number and left him her business card. She realized she would have to change the card and add her new married name. She smiled at the thought.

"Did you get a look outside, Pete?" she asked.

"Yes, but it looks like they left through the front door. I mentioned it to Keith. He said he'd check everything before he left."

The two left the shop and headed for Pete's truck. He opened the door for her, and she climbed up inside. He headed back to the station when they got another call on the radio.

"Unit 19, come in," the dispatcher said.

She grabbed the radio and keyed the mike. "This is Unit 19, go ahead," she said.

"We've got another robbery near your location. Can you copy?"

She flipped open her notebook and grabbed a pen. "Go ahead."

The dispatcher gave her the address and she wrote it down.

"We're in route, Unit 19 out," she said. Elena put the radio back in its holder and gave Pete the address.

He turned the truck around and headed to the new address. "It's only a block away from the first break-in."

"Two break-ins on the same day," she said.

"I wonder if we're dealing with the same people since it's so close to the other one," Pete said.

"That's what I'm thinking, too, Pete."

"That's what I like about working with you, Elena. We think a lot alike."

"I know. That's why I've been putting off telling the captain we're married."

He glanced her way. "You're thinking he'll separate us, aren't you?"

"I know he will. I just hope we're on the same schedule."

"I hope he doesn't leave you without a partner," Pete said.

"Yeah, me, too." She reached out and touched his arm. She liked touching him. It gave her strength.

Pete pulled up to the second store and managed to open Elena's door before she did it herself. She loved that about him—and the fact he once was an angel.

Elena grabbed the portable radio and clipped it to her belt. Then she touched Pete's cheek. "Thank you, Pete."

He helped her down and locked up. The two of them headed to the shop where the owner greeted them at the door.

Elena flashed her badge. Pete wore his on his belt.

"Are you the owner?" she asked.

"Yes. I went to open my store and realized it was already opened."

"What can you tell us about what's happened?" she asked.

"The door was pried open. The facing was damaged," he said. Pete looked over Elena's shoulder at the gouged-out wood.

The owner used some napkins to open the door for them. He led them to the register.

"Do you always leave the drawer open?" she asked.

"Yes, but the money is in the safe." The owner showed them to the office. "I usually leave the money locked in the safe over there." He pointed to a wall. A wall with a big hole in it.

"Oh, my. I take it that hole wasn't here when you left, was it?"

"No. There was no hole yesterday."

"Was anything else taken?" Pete asked.

"I don't think so. I haven't done an inventory yet, just glanced around."

Elena wrote down what the owner said, along with notes about the entrance.

"Did you see anything yourself?" Pete asked.

"No. I wish I had."

Pete took Elena's radio and called the tech team to let them know about this store as well.

"They'll be here shortly," Pete said. He clipped the radio to his belt.

"I guess we can wait until they get here," Elena said.

Pete shook his head.

"What is it?"

"I smell the same demon in this place," Pete whispered. He walked around the store, looking things over. "Can I see the office again?" he asked the owner.

"Help yourself," the owner said.

Pete remained in the office a few minutes, while she asked the owner more questions. "Did you recently hire anyone new?"

"No. I've had the same crew here for years. I pay them well so they will stay."

"Anyone acting different lately?"

He thought for a moment. "I don't think so."

"Anything unusual happen here, lately?"

He thought again. "I do remember a gentleman trying to sell me a security system. I have never had any problems before so I refused. He was very pushy."

"Do you remember who he was?"

"He left a card. It's in my office." The owner headed to the office to retrieve it and passed Pete.

Pete whispered to her. "The smell is the strongest in his office."

The owner returned with the card. About the same time, some of the tech team and a police unit showed up. Pete let them inside and they began working on the entrance.

"Do you have another entrance?" she asked.

"Yes." The owner led them to the back door. It was unlocked and ajar.

"Did you come in this way?"

"I did not."

Pete headed to the front of the store, while she looked around outside. The gravel in the back looked disturbed. She would have to alert the tech team to that fact. Before she could head back inside, Juan, one of the team members, joined her.

"We found some tire prints at the first shop. Since this is gravel, I'm not sure what we can find, but we'll get on it."

"Thanks."

Pete popped his head out the door. "We got another call." She joined him out front. The address was down the street.

"I'll walk," she said. Pete moved his truck to the end of the block. He waited for her and the two met the owner outside his door.

"That was fast," the owner said.

"Your neighbor down the street had a visitor as well," she said.

"Excuse us, just a minute," Pete said to the owner. He turned toward her, moving her away from the shop owner. "Elena, that demon smell is on you," he said. He sniffed her hair.

"On me? How did that happen?"

"Did you touch something in that last shop?"

She thought about what had transpired. "The owner gave me a card." She pulled it out of her back pocket of her jeans and showed it to him.

"Drop it."

"What? I need the information."

"Write it down and throw that card away. Do it now."

She pulled out her notebook and copied the name and phone number. Then tossed the card into a trash receptacle on the sidewalk. Pete handed her some sanitizer and she rubbed it on her hands, the pen, the front of the notebook, and a little in her back pocket. "Do you still smell it?"

He sniffed her hands. "I think you got it."

"What was that all about?" she asked.

"I wouldn't want him to track you. It's an overwhelming scent."

"Hmm." She followed Pete inside, where the owner had been waiting. Maybe it would distract him from any new demon scent, she thought. "Sorry about that," she apologized. She glanced around the shop. "What kind of store is this?"

"We sell parts for electronics, small appliances or small engines."

"Anything missing?" Pete asked.

"So far, just money from the register. If I'm missing anything else, I'll contact you," the owner said.

Elena pulled out her card and handed it to him. "You can reach us at this number," she said.

"We have a tech team down the street. They'll be here shortly," Pete added.

"Have you experienced anything unusual lately, besides this break-in?" she asked.

"Yes. I had a customer come in and suggest I get a security system. He was quite pushy about it and made me feel uncomfortable."

"Did he leave his card?" she asked.

"He wanted to, but I refused it. I didn't like the way he talked to me."

"What way was that?" Pete asked.

"Kind of threatening, like something could happen if I didn't get a security system in place."

"Do you think you would recognize him if you saw him again?" she asked.

"I think so."

"Our tech team has an artist who could draw him from your description," she said.

"Really? I would like to see if they can do that."

"Can you show me where this person was when you talked to him?" Pete asked.

"Right here," he pointed to the register.

"And where were you?" Elena asked.

The owner walked around to the register on the counter. "I stood here, facing him. He stood where you are," he said.

Pete reached out and touched the man's shoulder. "I want you to think about what he looked like when you talked to him."

"Sure. He said, 'it looks like you don't have a security system in here.'"

"And what did you say?" Elena asked.

"'I really don't need one.' Then he smirked and said, 'Yes, you do.'"

"Thank you," Pete said, removing his hand from the owner's shoulder.

"Do you have a back door?" Elena asked.

"Yes." He pointed in the direction.

"We'll take a look while we wait for the tech team," she said. She followed Pete out the door.

"I saw him, Elena. I saw the demon."

"Did you smell him as well?"

"Yes. The scent was strong in that spot."

"What kind of demon are we looking for?"

"He's passing himself off as human. He's good looking, sharply dressed. I'll have to reach out to other spirit beings to see who he is. I'm not familiar with him."

"How do we fight a demon?"

"This calls for a spiritual battle, Elena. I just don't know if I can protect you from him."

"There must be some way. Wouldn't prayers help?"

"Yes. You know how to put on the armor of God, right?"

"Yes."

"Do it now. We'll both do it." Pete closed his eyes in prayer, and she did the same thing, reciting Ephesians 6:10–17.

She made the motions, putting the belt of truth around her waist. Then she made the motion of putting on her breastplate of righteousness. She clicked her heels together to be ready to spread the gospel of truth. Then she made the motion of a large shield of faith that was as tall as she was, to put out the burning arrows of the evil one. Finally, she donned the helmet of salvation and raised her hand as if she held a sword of the Spirit.

"I'm ready," she said.

"We've got to do this every day," he said. He blinked and they were both physically wearing the armor of God.

"Wow! This shield of faith is heavy," she said. "And can you teach me how to wield this sword?"

"It takes a lot of practice, but yes, I will teach you," Pete said.

Just then, Amanda from the tech team came out the door.

"What in the world are you two wearing?" she asked.

"We're wearing the armor of God," Elena said.

"Okay? I need to photograph this area for Keith," Amanda said.

"Sure. It's all clear," Elena said. She headed toward the door with Pete following her. As they stepped through the doorway, he blinked, and the armor disappeared.

"Are we still wearing our armor, spiritually?" she whispered.

"Yes. I wanted you to see what the evil spirits see when we wear it," he whispered back.

"Oh. Well, that is cool."

She spent a few minutes updating Keith when her stomach growled. She glanced at her watch and realized it was after twelve. If she was hungry, she knew Pete was starving. She wrapped up with Keith and found Pete talking to the owner once more. Pete handed the owner her card. Since Pete was still new to the detective division, he didn't have any business cards, so he carried hers. That's another thing she would have to do once she spoke to the captain.

She waited beside Pete and when he finished, they walked out to his truck.

"Where are we having lunch?" she asked.

"Somewhere close. I'm starving," he replied.

"There's a sandwich shop over there. Let's try that one," she said.

They walked together across the street and went inside the Little Sandwich Shop.

There was a line at the counter. She glanced around the small shop. There were a few small tables with two seats at each one. Since there were many offices downtown, people must buy the sandwiches and take them back to work, she thought.

She noticed the menu was on a large chalkboard on the wall behind the counter. There were two women working. One was taking orders and ringing up the sales, while the other made the sandwiches.

"I'll take the ham and Swiss wrap with a bottle of water," Pete said. "How about you, Elena? What'll you have?"

"That sounds good. I'll have the same, please," she said.

Pete paid for their sandwiches while she watched the two women. The blonde woman ringing up their purchases had gorgeous skin coloring with a Mediterranean look about her. Her green eyes sparkled when she smiled. The Hispanic woman preparing the food was young and pretty, as well, but her eyes were dark brown with a beautiful caramel coloring. The two women joked as they worked, making it fun to listen to them.

"How long has your shop been open?" she asked.

"Oh, we've been here about four years now," the blonde said. "I'm Alona Gabriel, the owner," she said. "And this is my loyal employee, Teresa."

"Nice to meet you," Elena said.

"You haven't had any trouble here lately, have you?" Pete asked.

"No. Why do you ask?"

"We just worked three robberies in this neighborhood," Elena said.

"Worked?" Alona asked.

"We're detectives for the Miami-Dade Police Department," Elena said, showing her badge.

"Oh? No. We haven't had any problems." Alona handed her the two bottles of water.

"Thank you," Elena said. "If you have anyone asking you about security, would you call us?" she asked. Teresa brought their wraps to them, and Elena handed Alona her card.

"Do you want to eat here?" Pete asked her.

"Sure, why not?" They sat at a table with a view of the street. Another couple sat a table away.

Pete bit into his wrap before she could remove the paper from hers. "You really were hungry, weren't you?"

He nodded.

"This is good. I was hungrier than I thought," she said. By the time they finished, it was a little after one.

"We need to head back to the office and type up our reports," she said.

"Maybe Keith will have something by then," Pete said.

"I hope so. If we're dealing with professionals, it may be hard to figure this one out."

"Especially if a demon is involved," he whispered.

They walked outside into the Florida sunshine and crossed the street to Pete's truck.

"I didn't want to say anything inside the sandwich shop, but I felt the presence of a spiritual being of some sort," Pete said. He opened Elena's door.

"A spiritual being? Like an angel?" She stopped halfway inside the truck.

"I'm not sure. I've never felt that presence before."

She sat on the seat and put her hand on Pete's shoulder.

"But not a demon?"

"No. Definitely not a demon." He closed the door and walked around to his side of the truck.

"What have we gotten ourselves into, Pete?"

"I hope it's just a robbery, but I have a feeling it's more than that from what we've found out so far."

"You know, we may need to go back to the second shop, and have you touch the owner to see if he can remember the security hustler," she said.

"You're probably right. After we get these reports done, we can check back if we have time."

They each took a report and worked on it to finish faster. Then they exchanged the reports and added their own notes to complete them. The third one, they worked on together. Before they could finish the last report, they had another call. This one was a little different.

"This is a neighborhood not too far from downtown," she said. She glanced at the address, then handed it to Pete.

It was after four when they arrived. A police unit was already there. One officer stood outside a townhouse on the sidewalk. He kept the crowd of people away from the unit.

She showed him her badge. "Miami-Dade, robbery division," she said.

"What can you tell us, officer?" Pete asked.

"The couple inside were cooking dinner when two men barged through the door and accosted them. Officer Sanchez is inside, interviewing the wife."

"Did you speak to either of them?" she asked.

"I interviewed the husband," he said. He glanced at his

notes and repeated what he had written down. She took her own notes from what he had gotten, and wrote down his name, Officer Wentworth. "Thank you." She turned to Pete and realized he wasn't beside her.

When she glanced around, she saw Pete petting a brown dog beside Alona Gabriel.

Elena walked over to where Pete stood and said hello. She wondered why Alona Gabriel was at the scene. The dog stood between Pete and Alona.

"The Bensons are my neighbors. I live in that townhouse," Alona pointed to a nearby complex. "We closed the shop early today."

Relief washed over her. "Did you see anything?" Elena asked.

"No. I just heard the commotion outside and came to see what was going on," Alona said. She leaned over and petted the dog.

Pete locked gazes with Elena and then turned toward Alona. "Nice to see you again," he said. He joined Elena and they headed for the Benson townhouse.

"Would you interview the wife while I interview the husband?" she asked.

"Sure." Pete manifested a notebook and pen as they stepped inside the house.

Officer Sanchez greeted them at the entryway, and Elena showed her badge.

"Can I speak with you a moment?" Officer Sanchez said.

"Sure." Elena stepped back outside with the officer, while Pete went inside.

"They are refusing medical help," Sanchez said.

"Do you think they need it?" Elena asked.

"Yes. The husband has a black eye, and the wife may have a sprained ankle."

"Goodness. What else can you tell me?" Elena asked.

"The two were in the kitchen, preparing a meal when two white males broke into their locked door. They demanded money but the two are living on Social Security and had nothing of value in their home. They roughed them up and then searched their bedroom. It's a mess."

"Did they leave with anything?" Elena jotted down what the officer told her as she spoke.

"No. They left empty handed. At least that's what the Bensons think."

"You think they might have stolen something?"

"It doesn't make any sense, but the couple didn't see anything missing."

"Thank you, Officer Sanchez." She pulled out her card and handed it to the officer. "If you hear anything or think of something later, please let me know." *This robbery was sounding similar to those from this morning already.*

"Sure will." Sanchez left with her partner.

Elena approached the husband, who was in the kitchen, and began her questioning. He held an ice bag against his temple. She didn't see a black eye like the officer mentioned.

～

Pete spoke to Mrs. Benson in the living room. He had propped her foot up on a footstool and had placed an icebag on her ankle. "Is that better?"

"A little," she said.

While he placed the bag on her ankle, he healed her ankle. He was thankful he still had that gift. Mrs. Benson would think it was the ice. The same with Mr. Benson. After healing him, he left him with the ice pack for his eye.

"Tell me what happened, Mrs. Benson," he said.

"We were in the kitchen, cooking supper, when we heard a loud bang on the door. Samuel went to check. I heard some yelling and a loud thud. I went out and found Samuel on the floor. Then a man came out of our bedroom. I turned to run back to the kitchen when he threw my purse at my feet. I tripped over the purse, hurting my ankle," she said.

"What did he take?" Pete asked.

"I don't know. I haven't been in the bedroom since I hurt my ankle."

"Did you have something of value in there?"

"My jewelry," she said.

"Do you mind if I take a look?" he asked.

"Go ahead," she said.

He moved into the bedroom and glanced around. Drawers were pulled out and left open. Clothes were strewn across the floor. The closet door was open with clothes pushed aside, exposing a safe beyond the hanging clothes. The safe was still locked. Shirts were scattered on the closet floor. He needed to contact the tech team to see about getting fingerprints. He headed to the kitchen to check on Elena.

"Hi, Pete. We just finished here. Did you have questions for Mr. Benson?" Elena asked.

"We need to get the tech team here," he said.

She pulled out the portable radio and keyed the mike. "We need a tech team here at a robbery site," she said.

Pete motioned for Mr. Benson to follow him while Elena gave the dispatcher the address. He stopped in front of the bedroom door. "Mr. Benson, can you tell me what happened?" he asked.

"Again? I've already told my story three times tonight," Mr. Benson said.

"I understand. Is there anything you remember right now that you haven't told anyone before?"

"No. I don't think so."

"Why do you think the robber left the safe untouched in the closet?"

"Because I wouldn't give him the combination. That's why he punched me in the face," Benson said.

"Did he know about your safe before going in the bedroom?"

Benson froze. "Yes! He demanded I give him the combination for the safe."

"Have you seen this man before?" Pete asked.

"No. No, I've never seen him before."

"Hmm. Our tech team will be here shortly to see if they can get any fingerprints."

"Good. That's good."

"Tell me, Mr. Benson, did anyone speak to you lately about a security system for your home?"

"Yes. Just last week, a gentleman came to speak to us about a program."

"Can you show me where this man stood in your home, while you picture him in your mind?" Pete touched Mr. Benson's shoulder and focused on his eyes.

"Over there," Benson pointed to the sofa. Pete saw the

man Benson encountered, and he was the same man the shop owner had seen.

He walked over to the sofa and caught the faint scent of the demon he had smelled before. He felt a hand on his back.

"The tech team is on the way," Elena said.

"Good."

There was a knock on the door. Mr. Benson opened the door and it was Alona.

"Mr. Benson, I came to see if there was anything I can do for you?"

"Come in, come in. Yes. Anna and I were fixing dinner when we were interrupted."

"I would be glad to help you with that, if you want?" Alona asked.

"Yes, please," Mrs. Benson called out.

"Oh, my goodness!" Alona rushed over to where Mrs. Benson sat with her foot propped up and spoke to her.

Another knock on the door and Mr. Benson answered that as well. It was the tech team. Elena spoke with them briefly and showed them to the bedroom, where they got to work.

Pete watched as Mr. Benson and Alona went into the kitchen to finish preparing the meal. He checked Mrs. Benson's ankle and removed the ice pack. "Can you move your ankle, Mrs. Benson?" he asked.

She moved her foot side to side, then in a circular motion. "Wow. That feels much better. Thank you, detective."

Pete handed her a card with Elena's name on it. "If you remember anything later on or discover anything missing, please give us a call."

"Oh, I will. Thank you."

Pete went to join Elena and the tech team in the bedroom, to see if they had found anything useful from their work.

"They think they got some good prints on the safe and the dresser," Elena said.

He wanted to tell her what he discovered, but he waited until they finished up with the tech team. His stomach growled and he knew Elena was hungry, too. It was an hour before the team wrapped up and they were all ready to leave. By that time, Alona had also left.

On the way home, Pete broke the ice with his news. "I saw him again, Elena. He was there at the Bensons' home."

"Who are you talking about?" she asked.

"The Dark Demon."

"How do you know?"

"I touched Benson's shoulder and asked him to picture the man and where he stood. His scent was all around the sofa. His face was the same as the shop owner's vision."

"We need to look through the images at the station," she said.

"His image won't be there. He's a demon. He won't allow himself to get caught." His stomach growled again. He glanced at Elena. She pulled her phone out and dialed a number. He raised a brow. *What is she up to?* He kept his eyes on the road.

He heard her order a pizza. "Ah, yes." He hurried home, pulling into the driveway ahead of the pizza delivery. "Just in time," he said. He was able to help Elena out of the truck before the driver pulled in behind him.

After paying for their pizza, the two of them headed inside. It felt good to be home. He headed to the kitchen and grabbed a couple beers from the fridge and sat beside Elena at the kitchen bar. He handed one beer to her, and she handed him a slice of pizza. He bit in. "Hmm."

"All those robberies were petty in nature," Elena said. She bit into a slice of pizza.

"Except for stealing that safe," he said. He took a long sip of beer. Boy, that tasted good, he thought. It had been a long, busy day.

"Yes, except for that." Elena sipped her beer.

"Minimal damage was done in most cases," he said. He took another bite of his pizza.

"But they all happened on the same night," Elena said.

"And all were visited by the same demon." He held her gaze.

"How do we track this demon?"

"Do you still have his card with his name and number?"

"Yes, I do," Elena said. She took another sip of her beer.

"I guess we can pay him a visit tomorrow." She pulled out another piece of pizza from the box.

Pete reached into the box and pulled out another piece for himself. "Maybe we should pay him a visit before you speak to the captain."

Elena's heart sank. She dreaded that moment. The captain had noticed her change in attitude and asked her about it. She'd let it slip that she was engaged to Pete, even though they had been married a month now. She liked how things were going and enjoyed Pete's company on the job.

Pete touched her arm. "I don't regret anything, Elena. I hope you don't either," he said.

"Oh, Pete. I don't regret anything. I love working with you. I just remembered what it was like before you came along. I don't want to go back to that situation again."

He pulled her close and kissed her forehead. When they finished their pizza, Pete helped her clean up the kitchen.

"You know, there was something I forgot to tell you about the last burglary," Pete said.

"Oh? What's that?"

"I again sensed the presence of another spirit being as well as something else."

"Not a demon?" she asked.

"No. And not quite an angel, either."

"So, you think we're dealing with two spiritual entities?" she asked.

"Yes."

"Did you pick that up in the Benson house?"

"No. I sensed it around Alona and her dog."

She stared at him. Pete didn't lie, so it was hard to understand the implications of his statement. "What are you saying?"

"I think Alona and her dog are the spiritual entities."

She blinked, trying to soak in the information. "Alona is an angel?"

"I don't think so."

"The dog is an angel?"

"He could be shapeshifting as a dog."

"How do you know it's a 'he'?"

"It's a male dog."

"So, if Alona isn't an angel, what is she?"

"If I'm not mistaken, I think she's a Nephilim."

Elena locked the doors while Pete explained. "Thousands of years ago, angels came down from Heaven to mate with the women of Earth. God wasn't pleased about that and sent other angels to destroy the progeny."

"So, if she's a Nephilim, how did she survive?"

"That's a good question."

"Do you think we need to talk to her again?" she asked.

"She didn't have anything to do with the burglaries."

"Maybe not, but now I'm interested in her story."

"Me, too, but we'll have to wait on that." He pulled her into his arms. She hugged him back. She loved being in Pete's arms. His hugs usually grew into passionate kisses. This time was no different. As his lips pressed against hers, she felt his body react. Each kiss grew more passionate. His arms moved over her back, pulling her closer. When she came up for air, Pete bent and lifted her, carrying her into the bedroom. When he set her down on the bed, he smiled and blinked off their clothes. She smiled back. "I'll never get tired of that."

He climbed into bed beside her and continued his deep, sensual kisses, moving from her lips down one side of her body and up the other side. When his hands started to roam over her body, she was ready for him, but he tortured her by taking his time. "Oh, please, now," she said.

Pete smiled and continued roaming her body with his hands and mouth for a while longer until she called out once more. "Pete, please!" He obliged her until they came together in a climax that outdid all the others.

"You continue to amaze me," she said.

"Good."

The next morning was Saturday. Elena had two glorious days with Pete before she would tell the captain they were married.

"Your mother called while you were in the shower," Pete said. He set a plate of eggs on the bar.

"Thank you, Pete." He had prepared breakfast for the two of them. "I forgot tonight was our family get together.

You will meet my sisters and their families, along with my parents."

"Should I be worried?" He set her coffee in front of her plate and joined her at the bar.

"Just be yourself." She kissed his cheek. "Thank you for breakfast."

He took a bite of his eggs, while she filled him in. "We are a close family, but with all our different work schedules, we struggle to get together at least once a month."

"That's nice. Family is important."

"Mom was a dispatcher for the police department, and dad was an officer. They know the captain as well as some of the senior officers."

"Do your parents know we are married?"

"Yes. I told them right away because we were in Puerto Rico on the family weekend. I asked them to keep it quiet."

"What about your sisters? Do they know?"

"No. My mother hasn't told them yet."

"Are they in the department?"

"No. I was the only one who went into law enforcement, of the three of us."

"So, tell me about your sisters. What do I need to know?"

"Angelina is the oldest. She's married to a police officer turned lawyer, and they have three children. I'm the middle child and Catalina is the youngest. She's married to a lawyer and they have one child and one on the way."

"This should be an interesting evening," Pete said.

"Yes, especially if they start asking about your background. How much do you want them to know?" she asked.

"You can tell them the truth."

She put her hand on his back. "There's a lot about you that I don't know, either."

Pete picked up his cup of coffee and made another cup. "Did you want another cup?" he asked her.

"Sure." She moved next to him at the counter. He handed her the mug and took his in one hand and took her hand in the other.

"Let's go outside on the patio and I'll tell my story." Once they settled at the patio table. Pete hugged his mug. "I've been an angel for as long as I can remember. Before there were humans on Earth."

She touched his arm. "You don't look a day over thirty," she said.

"I trained Guardian Angels and warriors. Michael heads up the warriors and Raphael heads up the Guardians."

"Will you still teach me how to handle a sword?" she asked.

"If you really want to learn, we can do that later today."

"Did you ever have one of your trainees become human?" she asked.

"Yes. As a matter of fact, the last one I trained fell in love with a human. His name was Mike. I trained him to be a Guardian Angel. He saved the life of the woman he was charged with protecting and she helped him remember his past life and how he died."

"So, was he always an angel?"

"No. He was killed in the line of duty while working as a police officer. God had special plans for him and gave him a second chance, sending him back to Earth as an angel."

"Have you seen him since he became human again?"

"I got to be present at his wedding as his best man. He and María work in health care. She's a nurse and Mike is an EMT. He uses his healing powers in that field."

"Does he know you are now human?"

"No, but that gives me an excuse to contact him. I'll try telepathically and see if he can still hear me."

"Are they in the Miami area?" she asked.

"No. He and María live in Pensacola."

"Why didn't he go back into the police department?"

"It was too hard to explain to the people he knew when he was alive, so he chose the medical option since he still had the ability to heal."

"So why did you choose law enforcement?" she asked.

"I was sent on a mission to help you capture those two brothers. After training Mike, the Lord sent me on several missions to assist other angels or humans."

"Were you tempted to become human before you met me?"

"No. The other missions weren't as dangerous as yours."

"Dangerous? You thought my mission was dangerous?"

Pete nodded. "Remember all the problems we had? Your mission was the hardest one I've ever undertaken. And you're the only temptation I couldn't resist."

She stood up and walked around the table and sat on his lap. She wrapped her arms around his neck and kissed him. "You were my biggest temptation."

3

Elena and Pete arrived early at her parents' house. She was both excited and nervous. Pete held a bouquet of flowers in one hand and opened the door with the other, allowing her to step inside first. "Hello!" she called out. This used to be her home until she started working in the police department. After saving up enough to get a place of her own, she moved out. Elena clutched Pete's hand in hers and led him through to the kitchen.

"Are you nervous?" he asked her.

"Can you tell?"

He nodded. "I feel it through your hand."

When she walked into the kitchen, her mother was pulling two pies out of the oven. "Only two pies?" she said.

"Elena, you're early!" her mother said.

"Hello, Momma! This is Pete." She patted his chest. "Pete, this is my mother, Elizabeth Romero."

"These are for you, Mrs. Romero," Pete said. He handed her the flowers.

"Why, thank you, Pete. You can call me Liz." She wiped her hands on her apron and took the flowers. "Everyone calls me Liz." She pulled a vase out of the cabinet and filled it with water. Momma set the flowers into the water and wiped her hands again. "Now I can greet you the Romero way." She hugged Pete around the waist. Momma came up to Pete's chest. "Welcome to the family! I have three daughters and now I have three sons."

"What kind of pies are these?" Elena asked.

"Two are cherry pies and two are apple," momma said.

"Hmm, I can't wait to try them," Pete said.

"Where's Daddy?"

"Outside with the grill. Can you take these to him for me, please? I need to finish the potato salad." Momma handed her a small cooler with beer on ice.

"I'll get that for you, Elena," Pete said. He relieved her of the cooler and followed her outside. Elena wrapped her arm through his and led him to the back patio.

"Hi, Daddy! This is Pete. Pete, this is my dad, Raphael Romero."

"How do you do, sir?" Pete handed him the cooler.

Daddy took the cooler and shook hands with Pete, pulling him into a hug. "Welcome to the family, Pete," he said.

Daddy opened the chest and handed her and Pete a beer, then opened his own. "So, you two have been married a month and no one knows but Momma and me?" he asked.

"The captain knows we are engaged," Elena said.

Daddy opened the grill and checked on the chicken and burgers. "So when do you plan on telling him?"

"Monday," Elena and Pete responded together. "We wanted to tell the family first." Elena said.

"You've managed to keep this from your sisters, too?" Daddy asked.

"I just couldn't find the time," Elena said.

"We got married in Puerto Rico, just after the hurricane. By the time we got back, we barely had time to adjust to married life when we were back at work," Pete said.

"We wanted to get to know each other first," Elena said.

"How long did you two know each other before you got married?" Daddy asked.

Elena glanced at Pete. "A week?"

"A week! How do you know each other enough to get married after a week?"

"He saved my life, Daddy."

"And Elena saved mine a couple times. Besides, I'm a good judge of character," Pete added.

"Oh?"

"Yes sir. Besides, there's something else I need to tell you."

"And what is that?" Daddy turned the chicken over.

"I was an angel of God, sent on a mission to help Elena capture an exceptionally evil man," Pete said.

Daddy glared at Pete and then her. "You aren't joking, are you?"

"No sir. I crossed over during our investigation. I still have some of my gifts, but not all of them."

"And what gifts are those?" Daddy took a swallow of his beer.

"I can no longer teleport or go invisible."

"Neither can I." Daddy took a sip of his beer. "Tell me what you *can* do."

Pete put his hand on Daddy's shoulder. "Think about your first car, but don't say anything," Pete said. Daddy closed his eyes and thought about the car.

"It was a two-toned blue, 1959 Ford," Pete said.

"Yes, how did you do that?"

"I could see what you pictured in your mind."

"That must come in handy in your investigations," Daddy said.

"Oh, yes, it does," Elena said.

"What else can you do?"

"I can sense when there's an evil presence. I can heal people and call on spiritual help if we need it."

"He can also blink clothes off or on," Elena said.

Pete glanced at her, and she realized he had only done that when they were alone. "It could help when we're chasing someone, don't you think?" she said. She tried to recover from her blunder.

Daddy glanced at both of them. "I wouldn't volunteer that information in the future," he said.

Elena's face heated. "Pete's super strong, too," she added.

"I tell you what," Daddy began. "Let's keep this angel stuff as our little secret. You haven't mentioned this to your mother, have you?"

"No," Elena said.

"Good. The fewer people who know, the better, for your safety."

Pete nodded. "Sure," Elena said.

"The real problem will be with your sisters," Daddy said.

"Why is that?" Pete asked.

"Because you two have deprived them of a wedding. They were talking about what your wedding would be like the last time we had dinner together."

"Just think of all the money you saved, Daddy."

"Yes, thank you. I'm still paying off Catalina's wedding."

"Daddy, Elena!" Catalina called out. She came and hugged both of them. Catalina was followed by her husband, Juan, carrying their young daughter, Ellie.

Elena introduced Pete as her husband.

"I'm sorry, did you say husband?" Catalina asked.

"Yes," Elena said.

Pete and Juan shook hands. Catalina gave Pete a hug. "Don't think you're going to be off the hook," she said to Pete.

"What do you mean by that?" he asked.

"Catalina and Angelina will be asking you all sorts of questions," Elena explained.

"Here," Daddy handed Pete another beer. "You're going to need this.

"Thank you, sir."

"While I enjoy being called sir, you can call me Ralph."

"Ralph?"

"Yes, Raphael is Spanish for Ralph. I don't like the name Raphe, so call me Ralph or Rafael."

"Yes, sir, Ralph. Thanks," Pete said.

Catalina left to help Momma in the kitchen and Juan stayed behind to ask his own questions.

"So, what kind of work do you do, Pete?" Juan said.

"I'm a detective for the Miami-Dade Police Department."

"Oh, so you two work together?"

"Yes."

"I'm a criminal lawyer." Juan handed Pete his card. Ellie began to wriggle in his arms. "That's my cue for Catalina. I'll be back." Juan headed out to the kitchen to find Catalina.

"Help me carry this food into the house," Daddy said. He handed Elena a plate of burgers and Pete and Daddy carried in two plates of chicken.

Angelina was inside with Rick and their two daughters, Alicia and Reina, and Ricky, their son.

"So, when were you going to tell us?" Angelina said.

"Tell you what?" Elena asked. She tried hard not to smile as she set the plate on the table. She clenched her jaw tight.

"You know exactly what I'm talking about?" Angelina pointed a finger at her.

"How could you get married and not invite the family?" Catalina said.

Elena swallowed. Everyone stared at her, while they gathered around the table.

Pete touched her shoulder and pulled her close. "She didn't tell you because it was a spur of the moment thing. We were staying in a church in Puerto Rico, after the hurricane took out the house we sheltered in during the storm. I had been doing a lot of thinking during those few days and realized that I couldn't live without her. Since we were in a church, I asked the priest to marry us. All the other people sheltered there helped make it a memorable ceremony. Our phones were dead and we couldn't leave the island."

"We were working a case at the time," Elena added.

"But you waited a month before telling anyone," Angelina said.

"This is the first opportunity we had to tell you and we wanted to do it in person."

"That still doesn't let you off the hook. We're going to have a party to celebrate," Catalina said.

"Yes, a reception party," Angelina added.

"Oh, I like that idea," Momma said.

Momma sat the kids at their small table with their plates, while everyone else took seats at the adult table.

Pete kissed the top of her head and they sat beside each other across from Rick and Angelina.

"So, what do you do for a living, Rick?" Pete asked as he passed the bread.

"I'm a lawyer. I work with Juan in the same office."

"Good to know," Pete said.

"What did the captain say when you told him you were married?" Rick asked.

Elena and Pete exchanged glances.

"You haven't told him, have you?" Juan asked.

"We plan to tell him Monday," Elena said.

"How do you know about the captain?" Pete asked.

"I used to work for the police department as well. I figured I could make more money as a lawyer and went back to school while working at MDPD. I met Juan while I was at the department. I already had a degree in criminal justice. He guided me through the process and had an opening at his firm when I finished," Rick said.

"Are you two in the same division?" Angelina asked.

"We are currently partners," Elena said.

"Not for long," Rick said.

"Oh, you should be private investigators," Catalina said.

"I like working for the police department," Elena said.

"Me, too," Pete added.

"Angelina and I are paralegals. We both work at Juan's office, but we take turns. I work two days a week, now that I have Ellie, and Angelina works three days a week," Catalina said.

"And I work five days a week babysitting," Mrs. Romero said.

"It's not babysitting when you're the abuelita," Angelina said.

"It's still work and you two should be paying your mother something for doing it since it's on a regular basis," Mr. Romero said.

"You're right," Rick said. "And Angelina can cut back to two days, giving her mother a day off."

"Thank you," Mrs. Romero said.

"So, when are you two having children?" Mr. Romero asked.

Elena choked on her drink. Pete patted her back. "We'd like to be just a couple for a while before having children."

"Don't wait too long or you'll never hear the end of it," Juan said.

When dinner finally wound down, Elena walked outside with Pete and sat on the back patio.

"Here." Pete handed her another beer before sitting next to her. No one else was on the patio.

"What do you think of my family?" she asked.

"Very nice. They all love each other and get along. I like that."

"Yes. I didn't know my sisters were working for Juan's firm, but it makes sense. They can all enjoy vacations together."

Just then, Elena's father joined them. "So that's where you're hiding."

"Too many women in the kitchen," Elena said.

"So what do you do with your time now that you're retired?" Pete asked.

"Well, I've been retired only a little while. I'm thinking of starting another career," he said.

"And what is that?" Elena asked.

"I thought of becoming a charter boat captain and hire out for fishing trips."

"Sounds like a fun job," Pete said.

"I'm working on making some connections to see if I can moor a boat along the coast, before I jump into it."

"Have you already bought a boat?" Elena asked.

"No. I'm doing research now to see whether or not it's feasible and worth the effort."

"Well, let me know what you decide. That would be

great for you. You could fish when you're not busy." Elena said.

"There's a lot more to it than I initially thought. I contacted your cousin, Jimmy, to see if he would be interested in partnering with me."

"Why Jimmy?" she asked.

"Because he's young, just out of the military, and looking for a job."

"Jimmy is my father's brother's son. He also has a sister who got out of the military a few years ago," she told Pete. "How is she doing?" Elena asked her father.

"Adriana keeps to herself, but I heard she has a bar on Coconut Key called the Toasted Coconut," he said.

"You should check with her for a place to moor your boat. She may have connections there," Elena said.

"I hadn't thought of that. That's a good idea, Elena."

"Maybe we could try deep sea fishing and then tell all the people at the police department," Pete said.

"Well, this is wonderful. You are both very helpful. I'll keep you posted on how it's evolving once I get my license."

"That's great, Dad. You need something to keep you busy."

It wasn't much longer before everyone said their good-byes and headed home.

"That wasn't so bad," Pete said. They were alone in her car.

"I hope you had fun?" Elena asked.

"Yes, I did. I guess we can look forward to similar conversations with your family in the future?"

"Meaning?"

"Well, something Juan said about having children."

"Oh, yes. Daddy kept asking them when they were going to have kids. Angelina of course had hers first since she married first, but Catalina had been married almost five years before they had Ellie."

"And how long have Angelina and Rick been married?" Pete asked.

"About seven years. Alicia is almost six and Reina is three, and Ricky is eighteen months," she said. "I think Catalina is expecting her second child, but she hasn't told the family yet."

"Why not?"

"I don't know. She mentioned they planned on having their children three years apart and hinted around that she was pregnant without really saying anything. So far, she's not showing. By the next family get together, I'm sure she will be."

Elena pulled into their driveway. As usual, Pete got to her car door before she could open it.

"Thank you, Pete."

He pulled her into his arms and kissed her. "Let's continue this baby conversation inside." He kissed her neck.

"Oh, yes. Let's."

In another part of Miami, a crime boss waited on his subordinates for a meeting. Gustavo pounded his fist against his desk and stood up. "Where the hell is Carlos?"

"He didn't show up this morning, boss," Gustavo's assistant, George, answered.

"I need him to drive a shipment to North Miami."

There was a knock on the door. Jaime stuck his head in

the room. "There's something you need to see, boss." Jaime walked to the television and picked up the remote, turning it on. He scrolled through some channels and pulled up a local news program where the announcer was speaking.

"...the body of an Hispanic male was found outside a downtown parking lot early Friday morning. The owner of the parking lot was able to supply the police with footage from his security cameras. If you know anything about this incident, please contact the Miami-Dade Police Department. The number is on the screen." The next scene was Carlos, pointing a gun at someone. The audio was not available, but you could see he was talking, when something moved in front of the camera. It blocked the view. When the object moved away, Carlos lay in a ditch near the entrance of the parking lot. A few minutes later, two women walked past the area. One was a tall woman with light brown hair, the other a shorter brunette.

Gustavo dropped in his seat. "What the hell was he doing there? Don't I pay him enough to work for me?"

"Carlos had a side hustle of robbing people," George said. "I warned him about doing that, but he didn't listen."

"Jaime, find me another driver right away."

"Yes, sir." Jaime turned and left the room.

Gustavo sat, rubbing his forehead with his index finger. "Have the products been filled with the drugs?"

"Yes, sir, and the products have been loaded onto the truck."

"Raum is expecting a report on our security systems tonight."

"I have that, boss. Let me get it for you," George said.

Gustavo reached into his desk drawer and pulled out a bottle of antacids. He popped a couple into his mouth before George returned with the report.

"Here you go, boss." George handed the report to Gustavo.

Gustavo rubbed his forehead with his index finger. "Hmm." *Of the thirty-two businesses that were visited, Raum left a card with everyone. After our teams visited three businesses in the same area, two of those chose our security systems and another four signed up that weren't visited by our teams.*

"George, how far out are these security setups for the six businesses?" Gustavo asked.

"We've got them scheduled for one a day. We should be finished by next Friday."

"Schedule our teams to visit the next five on the list." He circled the five next businesses and handed the sheet back to George.

There was a knock on the door. Jaime stuck his head inside.

"I got your driver, boss."

"Go over the details with him, Jaime. Then follow up with him after the delivery."

"Yes, boss."

"Then call me when it's done."

"Yes, sir." Jaime left and closed the door.

Before Gustavo could say another word, Raum stood before him. "Oh, hello, Raum."

"Have you managed to secure more clients from my efforts?"

"We've gotten six new clients and we're working on the next five."

"You're working too slowly for my needs."

"Well, we've managed to capture more clients with the drugs."

"There's one client I'm particularly interested in," Raum said.

Gustavo motioned for George to bring him the list. When he handed it to Gustavo, Raum took it from him. He glanced at it, then set it on the desk before Gustavo. He pointed to one name.

"I want this business as the next client.

4

Elena and Pete spent the remainder of their weekend practicing with the sword of truth.

"How did you wield this sword in battle?" she asked.

"After a while, you'll build up your strength. Always remember to put on your Armor of God each day. Lift your shield." He showed her how to hold her arm.

"This will keep out the burning arrows of the demons."

Elena held up her shield while slashing through the air with her sword. "Can you give me the power to see these evil spirits?"

"Do you really want it? If I give it to you, I can't take it back."

"If you give me that power, will you lose your power to see them?"

"No. I will still have it."

"Then yes. I want to be able to see whom I'm battling."

Pete touched her head and uttered a prayer. "You now have the ability to see the spiritual entities, good or bad."

"How can we take down a demon, Pete?"

"That's a good question. We can hold them off with prayer and our battle armor, but to take them out of the game, we need an angel with shackles."

"Shackles?"

"To bind up the demon. I can call on Rafael and see if he can send us some spiritual help."

"Rafael, my father?"

"Rafael, the archangel in charge of the Guardian Angels. But if I'm not with you, call out to your Guardian Angel, Lia. She'll know what to do."

Pete blinked and the armor, shields and swords disappeared.

"Where did it all go?" she asked.

"We're still wearing it, but we can't see it or feel it. Just know that you have it on. When the time comes, raise your shield and sword."

Elena and Pete went inside, and she fixed them a meal of leftovers. They cuddled together on the sofa and watched movies the rest of the afternoon.

After watching a romantic movie, Pete kissed Elena's neck. When she kissed him back, one kiss led to another, until the two of them became one in a passionate climax on the sofa.

"I'm going to miss our weekends together," she said. Her legs were still wrapped around his hips.

"Can't we still be off on the same days?"

"The captain makes the schedules. But we can always ask," she said.

The next day, Elena and Pete headed to work in Pete's truck.

"We'll tell him together," Elena said.

"I hope we still have time to finish this case before he transfers one of us," Pete said.

"Me, too. I've got some ideas for following up on the security company," she said.

"Good thinking." Pete pulled into a parking spot and rushed to open Elena's door. She touched his cheek.

"Thank you, Pete."

They walked into the captain's office.

"Yes?"

Pete closed the door and joined Elena at the captain's desk.

"We'd like to inform you that we are married," Elena said.

"When did this happen?"

"Recently," Pete said.

"I thought you two were engaged," the captain said.

"Well, for a very short time," she said. It was true. *It was actually a couple hours before they tied the knot. But the captain didn't need to know that.*

"Do you know the statistics for a marriage lasting for a couple like you? A couple who hadn't known each other for more than a month?"

"Uh, Captain, we plan to beat the odds," she said. *And it was a week that they had known each other before they tied the knot.*

"Yes, sir. We've got a lifetime to get to know each other," Pete said.

"We'll see about that," the captain said. "It just so happens that Vice has an opening. Pete, report to Jenkins at 3:30 p.m. this afternoon."

"Can't we finish this case first?" Pete asked.

"Elena will be working that case. I suggest you go home and get some sleep. You'll be working graveyard a lot of the time, but Jenkins is coming in today with a report, so be here at 3:30 p.m."

"Yes, sir." Pete turned to Elena. "I'll meet you outside."

She nodded. She tried to keep her head up. *What a blow. Just like that and Pete was done working with her.*

"As for you, Romero—"

"It's Cummings now."

"Cummings, whatever. You'll be working alone. Again."

"Yes, sir. Is that all?"

"I guess you need to report to the HR department and change your status. Once that's done, I want your report on the downtown burglaries."

"I'm still working on them, Captain."

"Then I want a status report when you're finished with HR."

"Yes, sir." She left the room disheartened. Pete was sitting at their desks.

"I guess you'll have to ride home with me and get your car," he said.

"Yes, and we need to go to HR and officially change our status for our checks."

They went to the HR department and dealt with that for a while. When they finished there, Elena and Pete headed back to the house. She picked up her keys and kissed him goodbye. But his kisses always led to more kisses.

"I really have to go," she said.

"I'll see you at 3:30 p.m."

She blew him a kiss and headed to her car. While she drove back to the station, she thought about stopping by the security company. She pulled over in a shopping area to search for the address. She realized, all she had was the phone number. She continued to the station.

When she got there, she put everything down on paper

for the captain. She worked on an update for an hour with all her previous notes and reports. When she had it organized, she reported to the captain.

He sat and listened to what she had to say. "So, what's your next move?" he asked.

"I want to check on this security company. They came up in every investigation. I'm thinking they had something to do with the break-ins."

"All right but be careful. The new schedule is posted on the board," he said. He dismissed her. She headed straight for the board to check it out.

She still had Saturday and Sunday off for the next two weeks. Pete was off on Wednesday and Thursday and worked midnight to eight in the morning Friday through Tuesday. When would they be together? The captain did this on purpose. She would only see Pete in passing in the mornings. At night, he would be working while she slept alone. What a way to start a new life together. Her heart sank. One way or another, she would figure out a way for them to spend time together.

When she got back to her desk, she called the security company and asked about their services.

"Yes, we can outfit your business. Where are you located?"

"Downtown. I heard about all the break-ins. I want to prevent that from happening to me. All I want is an estimate and details on what equipment you will be installing."

"First of all, we need to know the square footage of your shop. We also need to see the shop so we can determine what type of equipment you will need."

"Don't you have some type of packages to choose from?"

"Well, yes and no. The packages are determined by the type of shop and the size."

"Let's say I have a retail store about 1400 square feet. What type of package do you have for that?"

"For a retail shop, we would put in several cameras with a monitoring system. The monitoring system can be set up in an office or at the register. Then we would install alarms for entrances and exits. How does that sound?"

"That sounds good. What would something like that cost me?"

"That all depends on the type of cameras you want and the number of cameras, how many entrances you have as well as whether or not you want the alarm system hooked up to the police department."

"Hmm. That sounds like a lot of factors I hadn't thought of. Let me get back to you on this. Who do I ask for?"

"This is George. You can call me Monday through Friday, 9:00 a.m. to 5:00 p.m."

"Thank you, George." She hung up. *It really sounded like they wanted to get into the business for some reason, before giving an estimate. She would have to call other security companies to see if this was standard practice.*

She dialed the first store owner who had been broken into for follow-up questions. He didn't remember anything new, but he mentioned that he bought a security system. He couldn't afford not to. Then she called the second shop owner. He made the same remark about getting a security system.

"They had the best deal after I called others," he said.

The third shop owner had set up his own security system. "I want nothing to do with that other company. I'll take my chances with my own system."

She thanked them all and decided to see what Keith found out at the scenes of the crimes.

"Hello, Keith. Got anything for me?"

"Hey, Romero. Congratulations. I heard you and Cummings tied the knot. Are you going with Cummings or Romero-Cummings?"

"Thanks, Keith. I think I'd like to use my new, married name."

"Sure. We did find some prints at all three shops."

"Great! Have you got any IDs yet?"

"Amanda is working on that. She should have something later today."

"Thanks, Keith. I'll check back with you on that." She left the office.

She had the Bensons to deal with yet. She decided to eat first and then call on them personally to see how they were doing and if they remembered anything. All she could do now was wait for Keith's findings.

She decided to head to the new sandwich shop she and Pete had discovered last week. She found a parking garage and pulled into it. It appeared to have some type of construction going on near the entrance. The last time she ate in this neighborhood, they had parked on the street. This time, all the spots were taken.

By the time she got to the shop, there was a line inside. The food was good, so it was worth the wait. Most of the people took their sandwiches back to the offices. When it was her turn, she noticed there was a table still empty.

"Hello, Alona," she said.

"Oh, hello, Ms. Romero."

"It's Cummings now."

"Cummings? Wasn't that your partner's name?" Alona asked.

"Yes, and now we're married."

"Congratulations! What will you have today?"

"I'll take a tuna sandwich on wheat bread with chips and a water."

"Coming right up," Teresa said.

"Is Mr. Cummings joining you?" Alona asked.

"Unfortunately, no. The captain assigned him to the Vice Squad."

"Why?"

"Because they don't want married couples working together."

"That's too bad. I...uh, never mind. I think if a married couple works well together, they shouldn't be separated."

"I totally agree with that," Elena said.

She paid for her sandwich and Teresa brought it to her, along with her water and chips.

"Thank you. I think I'll eat in here, if you don't mind."

She sat down alone, like she did many times before and ate her sandwich. Before she finished, Alona wiped down the empty tables.

"I plan to visit the Bensons after this to make sure everything is okay with them."

"Oh, I think they will enjoy the company," Alona said.

"Good. Well, thank you for a great sandwich, ladies."

"You're welcome. Come back any time."

She threw her trash away and headed back to the parking lot. Then she drove to the Benson house. Both of them were home and they offered her some coffee. She took them up on the offer.

"Have you two remembered anything new from the other day?" she asked.

"No," Mrs. Benson said.

"Have you caught the man who assaulted us?"

"Not yet. I'm waiting to get details from my tech team. They said they recovered fingerprints. Once I have those, I can cross reference them with images of the criminals. I may need you to come to the station to ID the man, just to be sure. In the meantime, you might want to contact a lawyer to help you with this case."

"Thank you, detective," Ms. Benson said.

"You're welcome. You two take care and I'll call you as soon as I get the word from the tech team."

She headed back to the station. Hopefully Keith would have what she needs to finish this investigation.

Pete wanted to surprise Elena by fixing dinner for her. He found her crock pot and had prepared some spaghetti sauce and left it on to cook. He got the noodles and set them out on the counter. It wouldn't take long to fix that. She could do that for herself. He prepared two salads. Maybe he could stop by for dinner, depending on what his new job would entail. He was disappointed in having to switch so soon without getting used to the idea of a job change, as well as a schedule change. Working from 3:30 p.m. to midnight wouldn't be too bad. He would at least get to spend time with Elena at night. He cleaned up his mess and set the table for her so she would know he thought about her. Then, he headed on to work.

By the time Elena came back from the Bensons, Keith had some information for her. He handed her the rap sheet for three different people.

"These are the prints we got from the downtown burglaries," he said.

"Three different people?" Hmm, she thought it would have been one person doing all of them.

"Yes, but check this out." He set the papers down. "The prints from the Benson house belong to this guy, here." He pointed to John Rankin.

She picked up John's rap sheet. Lots of robberies, nothing big. He had served time but not as much as he should. She looked over the other two. Eduardo Muñoz and Jorge Villa. Both had similar felonies. If we could keep them in jail, we would eliminate half the crime in the city, just like that, she thought.

"Thanks, Keith. I'll see if the Bensons recognize this guy." She held up John's paper. Then she headed back to her desk. A thought floated through her mind. What if she had a fake retail store downtown and hired the security company to put it in? What would she learn from that? And how was she going to catch these three men? She typed in the last known address for John and got a location in north Miami. Then she typed in the address for Eduardo and then Jorge. All three lived within a few blocks of each other in north Miami. Hmm. Maybe I'll take a drive up there and check out the neighborhood. She made some notes and then headed to the parking lot to get her car.

A red truck pulled in beside her car. She glanced at her watch. It was 3:20 p.m. "Pete!"

"Elena. I'm glad I caught you." He embraced her and greeted her with a sweet kiss.

"I love your kisses."

"Where are you headed?"

"I'm going to check out a lead. The three different suspects in the downtown robberies all live near each other. I thought I'd check out their neighborhood and see what I find."

"Be careful."

"I will. I'm wearing my armor, remember?"

"Yes. I cooked spaghetti for supper. You'll have to fix the noodles. I'm hoping I can get home to enjoy it with you."

She kissed him. "Thank you, Pete. I love you."

"Love you, too, babe. See you later." He squeezed her hand one last time and then let go.

They would make this work. They had to.

Elena drove to north Miami. Traffic picked up and it took a while to get there. She had put the address in her GPS and followed the directions. But the GPS led her to an abandoned-looking warehouse. The area didn't look very safe. She punched in Eduardo's address, which led her around the block to another abandoned building. When she plugged in Jorge's address, the GPS said 'address not found'.

"Great." She had the strange feeling she needed to get out of there, so she headed back to the station. With the traffic getting heavier, she didn't get back until after 5:00 p.m.

She would call it a day and head home. Tomorrow, she would have to come up with another plan. But the thought of setting up a fake retail shop came to mind once again. Where would she find the empty space to do this? Would the Captain even fund something like this? Or, maybe, she could find someone who would let her work for them and set this up to see what that security company was all about? There was something about them that needed to be checked out, but she couldn't put her finger on it. The fact that the business card smelled like a demon and that a demon had been present in all the robberies was not a coincidence.

Before she realized what had happened, she found herself driving through the downtown section of town, right where the robberies had taken place. She slowed her car as much as traffic would let her and glanced at all the shops on one side of the street. Nothing vacant on this side. She made a turn and drove around until she could go back in the opposite direction and view the shops on the other side of the street.

She passed the sandwich shop, then a couple more shops. Then she caught a red light. She glanced to her right. Next to the Martial Arts Studio was a vacant shop with a sign in the door. It read, 'For Rent.'

5

———

"**O**fficer Jenkins?" Pete said.

"Yeah? Who's asking?"

"Pete Cummings," he said. He offered his hand and Jenkins stopped to shake it. "The captain told me to report to you today."

"Really? That was quick. Come with me," Jenkins said.

Pete followed him into an interrogation room. Two other men sat at the table.

"This is Heins and Struber," Jenkins said. "Boys, this is Cummings."

Pete nodded and offered his hand. Heins shook hands with him and Struber crossed his arms over his chest and glared at him.

"Don't mind him," Heins said. "Struber doesn't like anybody."

"Then why is he here, serving the public?" Pete asked.

"I don't like bad people more," Struber said.

Pete scratched his head. *He hoped Struber was more helpful than he portrayed.*

"We're working a case that involves drug dealers," Jenkins said. "They're bringing in cocaine and distributing it somehow in the Miami area. We've got to find out where and when these drops are. We've had a few cases of children overdosing on the coke, so we've got to stop this," Jenkins said.

"When did these cases occur?" Pete asked.

"Yesterday. Two separate reports came in. One from the downtown area and one in South Miami," Heins said. He unfolded a newspaper and pointed to the article.

Pete picked up the paper and read it. "I say we interview the parents."

"It's already been done," Jenkins said.

"It might give us a clue where to start," Pete said.

"You're wasting your time," Struber said.

"Did the tech team go in there?" Pete asked.

"No. The children were brought to the emergency room and treated there. That's when they discovered the overdose," Jenkins said.

"I still think it would be worth going to interview the parents again," Pete said. "I want to see the room where the kids ingested the drugs."

The four men exchanged glances. "Struber, you get on the computer and find out what you can about the parents of both children. Heins, you find out what type of testing the hospital did and who was involved there," Jenkins said. "Pete and I will interview the parents."

Jenkins flipped open a notebook and glanced down the page. "Here it is. Let's go." Jenkins went out the door with Pete on his heels. Jenkins headed to a sleek looking, black Buick. Pete entered the passenger side and Jenkins, the driver's side.

"I really don't think this will amount to much," Jenkins said. "But I do have some questions about what happened."

After driving in silence for a while, Jenkins spoke up. "So why did you volunteer for Vice?"

"I didn't volunteer. I was in burglary with Romero. I got married and now I'm here."

Jenkins glanced at him. "So, the Captain is punishing you for getting married, huh?"

"I married Romero."

"Ouch. I bet she's hard to live with."

"She's easy to live with. I liked working with her. We think a lot alike."

"Is that so? I heard she was hard on partners."

"She's hard on herself. She felt she had to do everything herself because her past partners let her down and didn't do their part."

"Is that what she told you?"

"I saw it first-hand, plus, she saved my life."

Jenkins glanced at him again. "I heard differently."

"I bet it was from her past partners."

"You won that bet. How long did you two work together?" Jenkins asked.

"About a month. How long have you been in Vice?"

"Long enough. Vice wears you out, but you can't let it take you down. There are too many bad guys out there who need to be arrested."

"Are you married?" Pete asked.

"Was. It didn't last. Vice is hard on a marriage. My wife wanted me at home, at night. That's when the cockroaches are out, so what can I say? Someone's got to do it, right?"

"What about the other two?" Pete asked.

"Both divorced. Like I said, Vice is hard on a marriage."

Jenkins pulled into a driveway. "This is the first one. The name's Ivy. Their kid didn't make it." They both left the vehicle and approached the front door. Jenkins knocked.

A woman opened the door. "Yes?"

"Hello, Mrs. Ivy?"

"Yes." She glanced at both of them.

Jenkins showed his badge and Pete still wore his on his belt. "Miami-Dade Police Department, detective Jenkins and my partner, detective Cummings," he said.

"We'd like to ask you a few questions about your son," Pete said.

"Come in," she said. She wiped at her eyes and opened the door wider. She walked toward the living room and ushered them to the sofa. Her husband came to the living room from the kitchen.

"Supper's about—"

"We have company," Mrs. Ivy said.

"We were about to eat," Mr. Ivy said.

"We just have a couple questions," Jenkins said.

Mr. Ivy glanced at his watch. "Go ahead."

"How long was it before you realized your son wasn't acting normal?" Jenkins asked.

"When I got home from work, he was lying on the floor, listless. I couldn't rouse him," Mr. Ivy said.

"And where were you, Mrs. Ivy?" Jenkins asked.

"I was preparing dinner."

"Where did you find your son, Mr. Ivy?" Pete asked.

"In his room."

"Can we see his room, please?" Pete asked.

Mr. Ivy glanced at his watch again. "Okay, sure." He led the way to the bedroom. "We left it the way we found it. We thought the police would be back to inspect it, but they haven't returned," Mr. Ivy said.

Pete glanced around the room. Toys were strewn on the floor. It looked like the child had enjoyed his toys. "Where did you find your son, exactly?" Pete asked.

Mr. Ivy pointed to the floor at the foot of the bed. There were a couple of large plastic trucks and a stuffed white bear, something a three-year-old would play with. Pete squatted down beside the trucks and turned them over with a pencil he manifested. Then he moved the white bear and some white powder fell out.

"How long have you had these toys?" Pete asked.

"We've had the trucks for over a year but that bear is new. Where did we get that bear, honey?" Mr. Ivy asked.

"We were at a friend's house. One of Sammy's friends, Owen. Owen gave it to him the day before he—" she turned to her husband and cried into his chest.

"We will need this for evidence," Pete said. He manifested a baggy and placed the bear inside.

"Can we get the address of Sammy's friend?" Jenkins asked.

Mrs. Ivy wiped her face. "He's two doors down on the right." She pointed to the side of the house.

"Thank you for your time, Mr. and Mrs. Ivy. We'll let you know what we find out," Pete said. The two of them hurried out the door.

"We're going to Owen's house," Jenkins said.

"Why didn't the tech team check out the house?" Pete asked.

"I don't know. Unless the story was different at the hospital. Hopefully, Heins will find something we can use," Jenkins said.

They got out at Owen's house and approached the front door. Jenkins knocked at the door. A man answered.

"Yeah?"

"I'm detective Jenkins and this is detective Cummings of the Miami-Dade Police Department. We just want to ask a few questions about your neighbor, Sammy Ivy."

"The boy who died?"

"Yes, sir. Do you know anything about it?"

The man came out on the porch and closed the door behind him. "My wife and kid had Sammy and his mother over for playtime. Owen is three years old, same as Sammy."

"Did Owen give Sammy anything to play with while he was here?" Pete asked.

"Sure. When Sammy comes over, they both play with all of Owen's toys. When Owen goes over there, they play with all of Sammy's toys. That's how it works."

"Did Owen give Sammy a toy to keep?" Jenkins asked.

"Not that I know of. Besides, he would have gotten it back the next time he went to Sammy's."

"Could we speak to your wife about what happened?" Jenkins asked.

"No. She's upset about the whole thing. Had to see the doctor for anxiety. Her and the boy are sleeping now."

"Thank you, Mr.... uh what is your name, sir?" Pete asked.

"Denison. Owen Denison, Senior."

"Thank you, Mr. Denison," Jenkins said.

As they headed back to the vehicle, Pete got a bad feeling. He glanced at his watch. It was 7:15 p.m. *Something wasn't right.*

Jenkins unlocked the doors and they both climbed inside. As Jenkins pulled out onto the road, Pete spoke up.

"I don't have children, so I don't know about this, but what adult goes to bed at 7 p.m.?"

"A mother of a three-year-old might if he was rambunctious," Jenkins said.

"But would the three-year-old go to bed that early?" Pete asked.

Jenkins glanced at him and shook his head. "Something doesn't sound right, does it?"

Pete closed his eyes. *'I need your help, Rafael. Send some angels to look after the boy and his mother. Let me know if I can do anything here.'*

"You, okay?" Jenkins asked.

"I'll let you know later," Pete said.

"You know we can't do anything until a crime is committed, right?" Jenkins asked.

"Who made that rule?" Pete asked.

"There's nothing we can do here," Jenkins said. "We're heading to the other house."

"The child who survived?"

"Yes. Only this one is two years old. She won't be doing much talking."

After a thirty-minute drive, they arrived at the second address. "The name is Constant," Jenkins said.

Jenkins knocked on the door. A woman, holding a small child answered the door. She looked them over. "Who are you? And what do you want?"

"I'm detective Jenkins and this is detective Cummings of the Miami-Dade Police Department. Can we ask you a few questions?"

"I've already answered all the questions the police asked

me. Didn't they write up the report? They took a lot of notes."

"We're following up some leads," Jenkins said.

"Well, if you want a lead, you should speak to Jimmy Deeks, my baby's daddy. He's the one who brought home the coke she got into. I kicked his sorry ass out. Maybe he can answer some of your questions."

Pete touched her shoulder. "Thank you, Ms. Constant." He saw Jimmy, the way she saw him. He turned to leave.

"Uh, thanks," Jenkins said and followed him back to the car.

"We didn't get any information on Deeks," Jenkins said.

"I did."

"What do you mean, you did? Are you a mind reader?"

"In some cases, yes."

Jenkins headed back to the office. "You didn't take notes, did you?"

Pete manifested a notebook with notes in it. "Is this good enough?"

"I didn't see you write anything down."

"Didn't you?"

Jenkins' eyebrows furrowed. He tried to figure it out. Pete would have to be careful in the future. Elena was fine with his way of doing things. She understood him.

"I sure hope the other two got something on these people."

"Hopefully, they'll have what we need to connect the dots."

"I need to eat something. I can feel my sugar drop," Jenkins said.

"I fixed dinner for me and Elena. There should be enough left over for you as well," Pete said. He pulled out his phone and dialed her number.

"Are you kidding? Let's just pick up some fast food."

"Well, I made spaghetti and Elena loves my spaghetti. Hey, babe, is the spaghetti still hot? I'm bringing home Jenkins in a few minutes. See you soon."

"Uh, I'm not sure about this."

"We get a dinner break, right?"

"Yeah."

"There's no rule about where we take our break, is there?"

"How far is your place?"

Pete gave him the directions. "We aren't far now."

After about fifteen minutes, they pulled into the driveway.

"Hello, boys," Elena said. She opened the door before Pete could unlock it.

"How did you know we were here?" Jenkins asked.

"Pete told me." She smiled.

Jenkins glanced at him. "When did you do that?"

Pete touched his own temple.

Jenkins' brows furrowed again. He glanced at Elena and Pete.

"Telepathy," Elena said.

"Yeah? You expect me to believe that?" Jenkins said.

"How would you explain it?" she asked.

"He texted you."

Elena ushered Jenkins to the table. He sat down where she pointed and saw her phone sitting next to the place setting. It was opened to Pete's texts. The last one was from several days before. He picked up the phone and read it. "This doesn't prove anything," Jenkins said.

"Well, he didn't text me tonight, so it should," she said.

"Let him wonder," Pete said. He pulled her into a kiss. "This might be our last meal together," he said.

"I'll sit with you, but I already ate," she said. She went into the kitchen and brought out their dishes with the spaghetti and sauce on it. Then she retrieved some rolls and drinks for both of them. "So, what are you both working on?"

"Two children overdosed on drugs," Jenkins said.

"What?"

"One didn't make it, Elena. He was three years old," Pete said.

"What parent would let their kids get into their drugs?" Elena said.

"That's what we're trying to find out," Jenkins said.

"How is your investigation going?" Pete asked her.

"I checked out two of the three perps' last known addresses earlier, but it led me to a dead end, literally."

"Be careful," Pete said.

"I will. I just have to try to catch them somehow." She touched his arm. "But I have an idea about the security company."

"Oh?"

"I thought I would set up a dummy company and have them come and give me an estimate on putting in a system, just to try to catch them."

"Why would you do that?" Jenkins asked.

"Because the security company left a card at each business that was broken into," Pete said.

"Yes, and I think they had something to do with the break-ins," Elena said. She exchanged glances with Pete.

"Go for it," he said.

"Where are you getting the money for that?" Jenkins asked.

"I don't know yet, but I do have some money in savings. I just need an office space for a short period of time."

When they finished their meal, Pete was able to get another kiss from Elena while Jenkins used the bathroom. Then they headed back out onto the streets.

Jenkins finally pulled up at the police department. It was after 9:00 p.m. They found Heins and Struber working at their desks on their computers.

"Got anything for us?" Jenkins asked.

"The Ivys seem clean. Mr. Ivy works a good paying job so Mrs. Ivy could stay home with the kid. The Constants is only a Ms. Constant. Seems the daddy is missing. The birth certificate shows Jimmy Deeks as the father."

"We got that much from Ms. Constant."

"I can go through the books and locate Jimmy Deeks if you want to see what he looks like?" Pete asked.

"I'll save you the trouble," Struber said. He handed several pages to Jenkins. "That's his rap sheet."

Jenkins looked it over. "Drug habit of choice, coke, of course. Several arrests for theft to keep his habit going."

"We could pick him up for questioning," Pete said.

"Do you think he would tell us where he gets his coke?" Jenkins asked.

Struber and Heins laughed. *All he had to do was touch him while he questioned him and he would find out, but Jenkins wouldn't agree to that. He couldn't accept that he could speak to Elena telepathically when he wanted to.*

"I have my ways of getting to the truth," Pete said.

"Yes, and criminals have their ways of keeping it from you," Struber said.

"We forgot our evidence," Pete said.

"Damn. I left it in the car. I'll be right back." Jenkins left to retrieve their white bear.

"You found evidence?" Heins asked.

"Yes, at the home of the little boy, Sammy Ivy," Pete said.

"Didn't the police search the home for evidence?" Struber asked.

"No, because of what the hospital did," Heins said.

"And what was that?" Struber asked.

"The father rushed the child into the emergency room, so they listed him as unresponsive. They tried to revive him, but no one knew what caused his situation. He was dead on arrival. It was listed as accidental. Just before the article came out, the hospital reported the results of the blood test was an overdose of cocaine."

Jenkins came back into the room. "I dropped off the evidence at Keith's office. Hopefully, we'll find out for sure what the substance is, then go from there."

Heins explained to Jenkins what he had told Pete and Struber.

"If that is cocaine, then we'll need to question Mr. Denison again, won't we?" Pete asked.

"Yes, I'd like to know where that bear came from and who put the cocaine into it?"

"Denison?" Struber asked.

"It seems that Owen Denison, Junior, is the neighbor boy who played with Sammy Ivy the day he O.D.'d. He's the one who gave Sammy the white bear laced with cocaine."

"White bear?" Heins asked.

"Yes, we found it in Ivy's home. They left the room as they found it that night, but the police never investigated it because of what you just said," Jenkins said.

Pete got word from Rafael as Jenkins spoke. *'Owen Jr. and his mother had been drugged tonight. Their home life was not as it appeared. Their safety is at stake because Owen Sr. was very unhappy about his missing bear. His very expensive, missing bear.'*

'What can I do, Rafael? How can I help?' Pete spoke tele-pathically.

'You must save the boy and his mother. When Owen Sr. leaves for work, you must rescue Owen Jr. and his mother, or the two will die.'

"I have an idea," Pete began, "but you're not going to like it."

6

───────

Pete had explained his idea Heins and Stuber were parked a few doors down from the Denison house in a dark van with equipment to listen in on Pete and Jenkins, while they surveilled the home. The two sat in Jenkins' car a little further down the street, watching the house.

"I hope this pays off, Cummings, or we've wasted a full night for nothing," Jenkins said.

"Something isn't right in that house. You feel it, too," Pete said.

"We just got confirmation from Keith that the bear was filled with cocaine," Heins said in their earpieces.

"Shouldn't we go in?" Pete asked.

"No. We just watch for now. If Denison leaves, we check on the wife and kid, maybe leave a bug behind."

The surveillance went on for hours with nothing coming out of the house until morning.

"I see movement and lights on inside," Struber said.

Finally, the garage door opened, and a car pulled out.

Pete peered through his binoculars. "Looks like Denison is driving."

Once the car cleared the driveway and headed down the street, Jenkins gave the signal. He and Pete approached the house and knocked on the door. There was no answer.

"Do you suppose the wife and kid are with him?" Pete asked.

"That's a good question." Jenkins knocked again, only louder. Still no answer. "We'll have to find a way inside to check on the mother and son." Jenkins pulled out his radio as he walked back to his vehicle.

Pete remained at the front door and knocked again. He glanced over his shoulder, while Jenkins was busy getting backup, he turned the knob, breaking the lock. He waved Jenkins back.

A marked unit pulled up and two officers approached. Heins and Struber filled them in and then walked toward the Denison house. Jenkins joined him at the door and then they went inside.

The house was dark. Jenkins had his weapon out, but Pete didn't feel any danger. They found the mother and son, lying in bed together, fully clothed. Pete approached them and tried to get them to respond. He checked the mother's pulse.

"She has a very faint pulse. We need to get them to the hospital now."

Jenkins was on the radio calling for an ambulance. Pete checked the boy's pulse but couldn't find one. Pete touched both of them at the same time and prayed for their healings. Two EMTs came into the room and relieved Pete and Jenkins. Shortly after, the mother and son were transported to the nearest hospital.

"I think we need to leave someone here in case Denison comes back," Pete said.

Jenkins got on the radio and called for a team to watch the airport and ship lines. The replacement crew pulled up and Heins filled them in.

Once Struber and Heins were in Jenkins' vehicle, the four of them drove off and the other team took up residence in about the same location. Then Jenkins dropped everyone off at the department. "See you boys at eight o'clock tonight here in the parking lot."

Pete was exhausted. When he climbed into his truck, Elena pulled up beside him.

~

"Pete! Are you all right?"

"Hey, babe. We pulled an all-nighter. Looks like we'll be doing that again, tonight."

Elena hugged him and gave him a kiss.

"I've got to be back at eight tonight. I think Denison tried to kill his wife and son with drugs. See you when you get home." He kissed her goodbye.

Elena watched him get inside his truck and drive off. She already hated his shift, but what could she do? She headed inside to work on her cases. When she had everything up to date, she gave Keith a call.

"Yes, we got some good prints. Come on down and I'll show you what we have," he said.

She headed to Keith's office. "Here are the rap sheets for each of the prints. We got three good sets of prints for the shops downtown and two sets of prints for the Benson home."

"Excellent!" She examined the sheets and mug shots.

"Hey, these two, from the Benson home, are the same as two of the shop break ins."

"Yes. Muñoz and Rankin broke into the Benson home as well as two of the shops," Keith said.

She checked their last known address, and they were the same addresses she had visited with no luck. "These places don't exist," she said.

"That figures," Keith said. "They're laying low for some reason."

"Probably because they are into something illegal right now." Maybe she could sniff them out with a fake business? "Thanks Keith." Elena headed into the captain's office.

"What do you need, Romero?"

"It's Cummings, remember?"

"Cummings, yes. What is it?"

"I need some money for a fake business," she said.

"And why is that?"

"I want to see what this security firm is up to. I think they may have something to do with the break-ins."

"And why do you think that?"

"Because they tried to get people to buy their security system and when they didn't, the businesses were robbed. Two of them caved and got a security system in their business."

"And what kind of business are you thinking of?"

"There's a small shop for rent, downtown. If I could lease the space for a month and set up a retail type business and have the security system put in, I can see who is doing the work."

"What good would that do?"

"Well, if the people who committed the crimes are the ones setting up the equipment, I could arrest them."

"Do you actually think the same people would be setting up security systems that robbed the businesses?"

"It's possible."

"Find out what the lease is for two weeks and one month. Then we'll talk."

"Yes, sir."

She headed back to her desk and made some calls. The shop space was still available. The building owners would not lease it for two weeks, even for the police department, but they would do a one-month lease. The realtor handling the details gave her the dimensions of the space and invited her to check it out this afternoon.

She went to the captain with the information, and he put her off until he could speak with his superiors. She decided to do further research and talk to the recently robbed shop owners about their security systems.

Elena headed downtown and found a parking space in the neighborhood parking garage. She walked a block down the street to speak with one of the shopkeepers who went with the security agency that had left their card.

"Hello, Mr. Calhoun," she began. "Detective Cummings. I've come to follow up on the robbery last week."

"Oh, yes. We are back to normal here. The security company came in the other day and put the system in place. Let me show you," he said. He gave her a tour of his shop, pointing out where the cameras were and how he could view them in the office.

"Are you able to record things?" she asked.

"Absolutely," he said. He showed her how he could play back any recordings.

"That looks good," she said. "It would be very helpful to the police in tracking a thief."

"Yes, but I hope it doesn't happen again."

"Do you have any safety measures in place for a break in?"

"What do you mean?"

"An alarm system that would notify the police of a break in, in progress?"

"Yes. Let me show you." He led her to the front door and showed her where the system was put in place. "Once the alarm is activated, the police are notified while the break in is in progress, but the equipment will still be recording."

"That's wonderful. It looks like you are taken care of. Did you have any problems while they put everything in place?"

"The only thing that was odd was they insisted no one be here."

"Why is that?"

"I don't know, but they came in the next day and showed me everything they did and explained how to use the system."

"Oh, well, I guess it worked out just fine then," she said. *But what an odd thing to do. It seems as if they had something to hide by doing it in secret.*

Elena left and headed back to the next shop. After speaking to the manager there, he mentioned the same thing about not being there during installation. She thanked him and headed to the last shop, in which the owner installed his own system.

"Did you have any trouble with your system?" she asked.

"No. I did it myself with the help of my employees. It took an afternoon, but we got it in."

It was, after all, an electronics shop. It made perfect sense. She thanked the owner and decided to get some lunch before meeting with the realtor.

A few doors down, Elena was in the sandwich shop.

Alona and Teresa were there, along with a tall, good-looking man.

"Hello, detective Cummings," Alona said.

"Oh, you remembered me."

"How can I forget? I try to remember all my customers. What will you have today?"

"I'll try the ham and Swiss wrap with water and chips."

After Alona gave Teresa the order, she introduced the good-looking man. "This is Luke, our neighborhood martial arts instructor," Alona said.

"Oh, nice to meet you. I'm checking into renting the shop next to yours for an investigation I'm doing."

"Oh? What are you investigating, exactly?" Luke asked.

"I'm investigating a security company that left business cards at each of three businesses that were recently robbed."

"That is unusual," Luke said.

"You know, I may need to check out your facilities as well as the empty shop," she said.

"Why is that?" Luke asked.

"Well, this company doesn't want anyone present while they install their equipment. I find that very odd, and I'm stubborn enough to want to see what's the big deal."

"I don't blame you. Are you thinking they may have something to do with the robberies themselves?" Luke asked.

"Yes! It's like you read my thoughts." *'Just like Pete does.'*
'And who is Pete?'

She glanced at Luke. "Did you just say something?"

"No." *'But I did speak to you telepathically.'*

"Here's your wrap," Teresa said.

"Thank you." She took her food and sat at a table. She glanced back at Luke. *'Pete is my husband, a detective, and a former angel.'*

'I thought so. Come and see me after your visit with the realtor.'

Elena ate her wrap, trying not to think about anything while Luke was in the shop. Shortly after, he left the shop and headed toward his studio, a sandwich in hand. But she heard:

'I'm looking forward to seeing you again.'

Elena choked on her drink. What just happened? Was she imagining the conversation? She knew her conversations with Pete were real. The longer she knew Pete, the easier it got to communicate with him telepathically.

She checked her watch and realized it was time to see the realtor. She said goodbye to the two ladies and left the shop.

When she arrived at the empty shop, the realtor was inside. Elena let herself in.

"Well, this is it. You've got about 900 square feet of retail space, then back here, you have a storage room, access to the back door, two bathrooms, and a small kitchenette for employees or a break room," she said.

"This all looks great, but what if I want to put in a security system?"

"What do you mean?"

"Do I have access to an attic or anything like that?"

"Why would you need that?"

"I'm not sure I do, but if I'm asked, I need to know what the limits are."

"Well, if anything needs to be fixed that's in the ceiling, we would need to be notified, other than changing out the florescent bulbs."

"I understand. Thank you."

"So, are we good? Will you be leasing this space?"

"Let me check with my captain. Can I contact you before the day is out?"

"Yes. We'll have to sign a contract and I will get the keys to you."

"Okay. I will let you know something before 5:00 p.m. today."

Elena left and went next door to Luke's martial arts studio.

"He's teaching a class, but he will be done, shortly. You can wait over there," the receptionist said.

Elena sat down on the sofa and called the captain.

"Sorry, Romero. We can't handle the lease," the captain said.

"Yes sir." She shut off her phone. *He still called her Romero. Was he trying to imply something?*

Thoughts flowed through her head about the investigation, the security company, the criminals committing the crimes, and the department. She was surprised when Luke stood before her.

"Come to my office," Luke said. He reached out a hand to help her off the sofa.

"Wow, I was sunk into the seat," she said.

"It happens to everyone. It's temporary seating anyway."

After they walked into his office, he ushered her to a seat. "Now, we can talk."

"How is it you are telepathic?" she asked.

"If Pete was a former angel, didn't he tell you about me?"

"What do you mean?" she asked.

"I thought he would have mentioned I am an angel as well."

"Wait, he told me Alona's dog was an angel," she said.

Before her eyes, he transformed into a large brown dog, leaning on the desktop.

She stood up. "Well, in that case, he was right," she said.

Luke transformed into a human again.

"So, does Alona know?"

"No, not yet. And I want to keep it that way for now."

"Why are you telling me this?"

"Because I need an ally and so do you."

"How can I help you?"

"Alona is being tracked by a demon, but she doesn't know that. I can only watch out for her when I'm physically present. My presence in this studio is only temporary, so I can be near her during the day."

"How can I possibly help you?"

"You can be my eyes and ears here, while I search for the demon."

"My captain won't allow me to lease the shop next door, otherwise, I could help you."

"I will work something out for you. This dark demon must be stopped, and only by an angel. What you want to do will give you the information you need to pursue your investigation."

"Okay, what's the first step?"

"Tell the realtor you'll take the shop. I will work on your captain. There are things I can do in the day if you are watching out for Alona. You know she is a Nephilim, right?"

"Uh, well, Pete mentioned that she might be. What exactly is that?"

"She's half angel and half human. I'm trying to teach her how to use her humanness to protect herself and others, rather than her Nephilim self. She's very strong and can sense a demon, but the way she responds will get her arrested and exposed."

"Okay, I'll speak to the realtor about the shop."

"Remember, this is our secret. Alona must not know. Not yet."

"Can I tell Pete?"

"He is the only one you can tell, but no one else."

"All right, and you will continue to keep me informed?"

"Yes, we will speak telepathically from here on out."

Elena called the realtor and met her at the shop. There, she signed the papers. Before she made a payment, she heard from the captain. "The department will pay the lease for one month only. You better show some results, Romero."

"Yes sir, and it's Cummings, remember?"

"Whatever, just get me some results."

"Yes, sir."

She worked out the details with the realtor and took the keys. Then she made another stop at the martial arts studio.

Luke was still there. "Luke, you would save me a lot of time if I could get you to oversee the installation of the security system. I need to know what they are hiding when they install it."

"Make the appointment and I'll be there. Just let me know the time and date."

"Thanks." Elena headed out to the parking lot. She heard some familiar voices and turned to see Alona and Teresa walking in her direction.

"Oh, hello," Elena said.

"What are you doing here?" Alona asked.

"Well, I guess we will be downtown neighbors for a while," she said.

"How is that?"

"I was able to lease the shop next door to the martial arts studio."

"Oh? That's where Luke works," Alona said.

Elena heard a hammer on a gun being cocked. "Hold it right there, ladies," a male voice said.

Elena reached for her concealed weapon, under her shirt, and felt cold steel against her back. "I wouldn't do that if I was you." Suddenly, everything went dark. A bag shoved over her face allowed her to breathe, but she couldn't see anything. It smelled like wool. Her hands were pulled behind her back and restrained. She could feel her weapon being removed from its holster. The sound of screeching tires came closer. Someone shoved her around until she felt thrown against cold metal. Something heavy was shoved against her twice. Then a door slammed shut, cramming her legs against her chest. The sound of muffled voices came from beside her. She felt as if she was inside a vehicle, she felt movement.

'Luke, something is happening right now. I've been kidnapped, but I don't know where Alona and Teresa are. They were standing beside me when it went down.'

Then she concentrated on Pete. *'Pete, if you can hear me, I'm being kidnapped from a downtown parking lot. I was with Alona and Teresa when it happened. I love you!'*

She felt herself being tossed around in her confined spot. It felt like the back of a vehicle. She dared not talk. She let her senses take in what was happening.

"Ouch!" a female voice called out.

"Alona? Is that you?" *Teresa's voice?*

"I'm here, too," Elena said.

There was a sharp turn and all three of them slid into each other. "Sorry," Elena said.

The vehicle stopped abruptly. The doors opened. Someone pulled her arm, yanking her out of the vehicle. She was unsteady on her feet but felt another body bumping into her.

Suddenly, her hood was yanked off. The bright lights blinded her. She made out Alona and Teresa standing with her. Their hands were bound as well. Three men stood before them, wearing ski masks. One appeared to be wearing her service weapon.

"He wants this one," the tallest reached for Alona's arm and pulled her toward him.

"What about these two?" another asked.

"Just hold them until told otherwise," the tall one said.

'Great. Luke, can you hear me? We're in some type of warehouse. We're probably still in Miami. Someone took Alona. I'm not sure what they plan for us, but it doesn't look good.'

'Picture the inside of the warehouse. I will find you.'

'My Guardian Angel is Lia. And Lia, I can use your help right now.'

7

―――――

While Elena stood beside Teresa, she tried to get out of her restraints, with no luck. She glanced around the warehouse and pictured it for Luke. There were a couple of eighteen-wheelers inside, with pallets of cardboard boxes stacked near the rear of each truck. That end of the warehouse was closed with two giant doors where the trucks must have entered. The end where she stood had a large opening. Near the opening, the white van they arrived in sat parked. There were two rows of tables with four tables in each row, between where they stood and the white van. It appeared to be some sort of production area, with stacks of cardboard under the tables.

She hadn't heard from Pete. Was he still sleeping? She heard some crashing noise, like furniture being tossed around. The two men guarding her and Teresa glanced in the direction of the noise.

"Go check it out," one said to the other. The man with a blue ski mask went into the office. She thought about rushing the last man, but she had no hands free to retrieve her weapon. Suddenly, there was another crashing sound.

"Damn it!" The last man ran toward the office. She nudged Teresa and the two of them ran toward the opening where the van was parked. There was the sound of running footsteps coming from behind them. When Elena glanced over her shoulder, there was Alona.

"How did you escape?" she asked Alona.

"Hold still," Alona grabbed the rope Elena was tied with and pulled. The rope fell away. She handed Elena her weapon. Elena rubbed her wrists after putting her weapon back into her holster.

Alona freed Teresa the same way, breaking the rope in two. "Let's get out of here," Alona said.

"Is someone going to tell me what's happening?" Teresa asked.

"I escaped, that's all you need to know," Alona said.

Before the three of them got very far, a large red truck pulled up in front of them.

"Pete! It's Pete," she said. But there was someone else with him.

"Luke?" Alona said.

Both men got out of the truck and walked toward them.

"How did you know we were here?" Alona asked Luke.

Elena embraced Pete who picked her up and squeezed her tight.

"We need to call this in," Elena said.

"No!" Alona said. "We need to leave this place. Now!"

"Alona, they need to do their job," Luke said. "Tell me what happened." Luke put his arm around Alona. "Please, Alona, tell me."

"There were three of them at first. One shoved me into a seat. Another one got in my face and threatened me, but the third one slapped me and threatened me. I lost it. I tore my ropes off and grabbed my chair and beat them with it."

"Did you even try the moves I showed you?" Luke asked.

"It happened so fast. I just reacted without thinking."

"We'll work on that, but are you okay?"

"Yes. I'm just angry right now."

Pete pulled out his radio and called the dispatcher and gave the dispatcher the address. It dawned on Elena that she had driven through this area before, when she heard Pete give out the address. This looked like the neighborhood of the perps from the downtown robberies.

Pete tried to calm Teresa. Elena took some deep breaths to help relieve the stress from her recent ordeal. Alona also tried to comfort Teresa. Both Alona and Pete's efforts paid off, and it helped her own jangled nerves. She had not been on this end of things since she and Pete teamed up in Puerto Rico.

"We'll get you girls back to the parking garage when we finish here," Pete said.

"What are we waiting for?" Teresa asked.

A police cruiser showed up then. "They will have questions for us all before we can leave," Pete said.

"I've got to get home to my dog," Alona said.

"Trust me, Alona, he will be fine," Luke said.

Another cruiser pulled up and the police approached the small group. Two officers started the questioning, while another two went inside the office to investigate.

Alona was questioned the longest, then Teresa and finally Elena got interviewed. Pete and Luke didn't spend much time at all in their interviews. During that time, a couple of ambulances pulled up, along with a set of detectives from North Miami.

Since she and Pete were both detectives, they went with an officer and one of the detectives to the office. It looked like a tornado went through the room. There were bodies everywhere. A tech team was inside, photographing every-thing and collecting evidence.

Besides the broken chair, the desk was broken in half, another chair was splintered all over the floor. The window had a body hanging half inside and half outside.

An EMT approached their detective. "All the bodies are deceased."

"What in the world did this?" the officer asked.

Pete glanced at her. "I'd say it was self-defense."

"Where's the evidence of that?" the officer asked.

She glanced up at the ceiling. "I'd say you may have video evidence of what happened here." She pointed to the camera facing the desk. The detective took notes and finally led her and Pete back to the group. Elena handed the detec-tive her card and he gave her his card.

After the small group loaded up in Pete's truck, he drove them all back to the parking garage. He made sure everyone was safely in their vehicle before walking her to her Mustang.

"I'll meet you at home," she said.

Pete wrapped his arms around her and gave her a tender kiss. "You gave me a real scare today," he said.

"We have a lot to talk about," she said.

She drove home, going over the events in her mind. The ordeal shook her to her core. Teresa and she could have been killed, but what had Alona gone through to make her fight back like she did? And the strength Alona possessed was enormous. She hoped those cameras proved it was self-defense.

Then she wondered what that warehouse was being used for. There had been a couple of eighteen-wheelers inside, but what was inside of them? Or what was inside those boxes? She would have to wait to get those answers.

This was North Miami. She pulled over into a gas station and called the captain. He had already gone for the day. She would see him tomorrow and fill him in.

As she continued the drive home, she thought about why those men were looking for Alona. Were they connected to this demon? Somehow, she would contact Luke and find out what he knew. He may have the answers she needed. When she pulled into her driveway, Pete's truck was already there.

She found him inside. He had already pulled out leftovers from the fridge. When he saw her, he gave her another hug. "This wouldn't have happened if I was with you," he said.

"I think you're right, but I think they were looking for Alona. They said as much. Teresa and I just happened to be in the way."

Pete pulled out a couple of dishes and put food on each plate, while she poured each of them a drink. Then Pete put a plate in the microwave.

"How did you and Luke manage to find each other?" she asked.

"I heard you telepathically and headed out. Before I responded, Luke contacted me telepathically. He said he would join me. Then, he was in the truck. He explained what he told you and we discussed some things about your cases."

"I wasn't sure if you heard me," she said.

Pete handed her a plate and set his inside the microwave. *Our telepathic skills will increase the more we use them,* he said, telepathically.

Is that so? She pictured her and Pete naked and in bed.

Pete turned and smiled. Shortly after their dinner, they were cuddled together in bed, just as she envisioned.

"How's your investigation going?" she asked him.

"We're still on a stakeout tonight, watching for Denison to return."

"Didn't you tell me he tried to kill his wife and son?"

"Yes. I hope to check on her tonight and see how she's doing. Maybe she can talk."

She watched him stiffen. "What is it?"

"I just got a word from Rafael."

She waited for him to speak, touching his arm to comfort him. This didn't sound good. "Pete?"

"Mrs. Denison and the boy didn't make it." Pete clenched his jaw.

She sat up and hugged him. "I'm so sorry, Pete."

He rubbed her back. "I hate when an innocent child dies."

"Me, too."

The two of them cuddled a while longer until Pete had to get ready for work.

She picked up a book she had been reading since Pete was transferred to the Vice Department. She started where she had left off, reading a page or two before Pete was dressed and ready to go. He sat on the edge of the bed and kissed her.

She returned the kiss. "It's so easy to love you. You never complain. I can't seem to get enough of you," she said.

"I wish I didn't have to go in tonight. It's tough leaving you." Pete glanced at his watch. "I've got to go!" He rushed to the door, turned, and winked. "Love you, babe."

"Love you, too."

~

Pete met with Jenkins and together, they headed to the stakeout.

"I'm afraid it's too late for Mrs. Denison and little Owen," Pete said.

"How do you know? Did you call the hospital?" Jenkins asked.

"No. I get my information through other sources."

When they relieved the other team, the news wasn't good. "No one has come or gone all afternoon," Heins said.

"What about this morning?" Pete asked.

"Same thing," Struber said. "No one in or out."

"Any lights come on or go off?" Jenkins asked.

"There's only the one that's been on the whole time," Heins said. "Besides, with no one there, why would they?"

Pete and Jenkins sat in the car. Pete called the hospital and asked to speak to the head nurse for any information. "Nothing? Not even a word?" he asked.

"Neither of them regained consciousness."

Nothing happened for some time. "I don't like the feeling I'm getting about all this," Pete said.

Jenkins scrolled through his phone for news feeds. "Oh, yeah? What feeling is that?"

"I think Denison is involved in the distribution of these bears somehow."

"What the hell?" Jenkins stared at his phone. Pete glanced over. It was the story about the warehouse in North Miami. It showed the interior of the office without the bodies.

"Elena was there," Pete said.

"What do you mean?" Jenkins asked.

"She and two other women were kidnapped and brought there."

"Who did this?" Jenkins pointed to his phone.

"One of the young women. It was self-defense."

"Bullshit! One woman did all this damage. With five dead bodies?"

"If I told you the truth, you wouldn't believe me."

"Try me."

"Do you believe in angels?" Pete asked.

"I've had some close calls, so yeah. Why?"

"The woman who did all that damage is a Nephilim."

"A what?"

"Nephilims are half angel and half human. They were believed to be wiped out."

"You're telling me a thousand-year-old woman who is half-angel and half-human did this?"

"Well, she would be more like two thousand now, and yes."

"How do you know this?"

"Because I was once an angel myself." Pete clenched his jaw. He had said more than he had planned.

Jenkins sat back in his seat and studied him. "Why aren't you an angel anymore?"

"Because I fell in love with Elena. I can't be part of this world and heaven at the same time. I made a choice to remain with Elena."

"Do you have any powers?"

"Some."

"Like what?"

The sound of a car made Pete freeze. "He's back."

"Who?"

"Mr. Denison." They watched his car pull into the driveway. The garage door raised and Denison pulled in and the door closed.

"There was only one person in the car," Jenkins said. He pulled his binoculars away from his face. Fifteen minutes passed before the garage door opened once more and the car emerged. When the garage door was closed again, Mr. Denison drove away.

"Let's see where he is going," Jenkins said. He started his car and moved slowly down the street. He followed at a good distance.

Pete radioed for another unit to stand by. They continued to follow Denison's vehicle to the airport. Pete called the dispatcher again to alert the unit standing by where they were.

Jenkins parked the car and they followed Denison until he walked up to a ticket line. Before he could leave the counter, Pete touched his shoulder.

"Hello, Mr. Denison. I was wondering how your wife and son are doing right now."

Denison froze and his eyes widened. Pete saw the vision Denison had of the two he left behind. He pulled Denison's arm up and behind his back. "You are under arrest for the murder of your wife and son," Pete said.

Jenkins clamped the cuffs on Denison, while Pete ushered him away from the counter. Jenkins grabbed Denison's suitcase and radioed for another unit.

Denison kept eyeing his suitcase but didn't respond. The three of them made it to the front of the airport, where a police unit pulled up. Once Denison was searched and inside the cruiser, they opened his suitcase. Inside, there were several white bears and some clothes. Rolled up in his toiletry bag was a lot of cash in hundred-dollar bills. Denison's ticket was for South America, one way.

Denison was taken to jail by the other officers, but Pete and Jenkins had to meet them there to process Denison. Denison refused to talk. Pete put his hand on Denison's shoulder once again. "Can you tell me where those bears came from, Mr. Denison?"

"I'm not telling you anything," Denison said. But his thoughts went straight to the warehouse where the bears were assembled with the cocaine baggies inside. The same warehouse Elena and the girls had been taken to earlier. Pete squeezed his shoulder.

"Then tell me where these bears go after they leave your warehouse?"

Denison's eyes grew large. "What warehouse? What are you talking about?" This time, his thoughts went to department stores in North Miami.

"Thank you, Denison, for your cooperation." Pete took his hand off Denison's shoulder.

He glanced at Jenkins. "I got what we needed." After processing Denison, the two headed to Jenkins' car. Jenkins gave Pete the radio and Pete called for another unit to meet them at the warehouse in North Miami.

"He showed me where these bears are assembled and where they are taken afterward. Let's go."

The two drove off in Jenkins' car. "How did you know about the wife and kid?" Jenkins asked.

"While you were watching news feeds of the trashed office in North Miami, I called the hospital, remember?"

"Oh, yeah."

"When I asked him about the wife and son, he pictured them as he left them and I could see him injecting both of them with drugs."

Pete gave Jenkins the first address. "Mr. Denison buys cheap bears and inserts the baggies into the bears and sews them back up. This takes place in the warehouse where Elena had been taken. Then, these bears are packed in boxes and taken to the department stores, where they are sold to special clients."

When the two arrived at Denison's warehouse, the backup unit was already there. The place had been cordoned off. They opened a box near the rear of the eighteen-wheeler. Inside the box were white bears. Pete pulled one out and carefully cut the seam down the back with a pocketknife. A plastic zip-lock bag containing a white substance fell out.

Finally, the North Miami tech team showed up. Pete handed them the bear and baggie. While the tech team did their job, Pete and Jenkins walked around the warehouse. Pete took pictures with his phone. They found other evidence as well as a list of deliveries on the seat of one of the trucks to Miami Beach, North Miami and South Miami.

The cardboard boxes stacked inside the trucks were opened by the tech team and the North Miami officers. Inside each box were twenty-five white bears. Inside each bear they retrieved a baggie with a white substance inside it. Pete took more pictures.

"Now all we need is to check out these locations and we can put everyone out of business," Jenkins said.

They headed back to the office to write up their reports and get set up to make the arrests at the businesses in question. By now, it was around 5:00 a.m. The arrests would be made in a raid when the businesses opened. By the time the reports were done, it was about 7:00 a.m. They couldn't make the arrests until 9:00 a.m. when the businesses were opened. They would meet with the captain at 8:00 a.m. and set everything up for a raid of sorts.

"Let's grab a bite to eat before meeting with the captain," Jenkins said.

"Great idea! I'm starved," Pete said. Jenkins drove them to the nearest Waffle House.

"I should call Elena about this," Pete said.

"Why? This is our bust."

"Yes, but it ties into what happened to her yesterday. Plus, I think the perps from her robberies lived in that area."

"Why don't you tell her after the raid?" Jenkins asked.

"I like to share my good news with her and she shares hers with me. Didn't you do that with your wife?"

"No."

"That's too bad."

Pete ordered a big breakfast and so did Jenkins. They didn't have much to talk about other than this case and there was not much to say about it anyway. He wished he was still working with Elena. Just talking about their cases helped to figure things out.

Before they left the restaurant, Pete got a call from Elena.

"Hey babe, what's up?"

"I was just checking on your stakeout. How did it go?"

"We caught Denison trying to leave the country. Plus, the warehouse you girls were taken to is where the drugs were sitting, boxed up little white bears stuffed with cocaine."

"In the semi-trucks?"

"Yes."

"I need to call the North Miami detectives and see if they identified the suspects."

"Why is that?"

"Because it just might prove my theory," Elena said.

"What theory?"

"That the perps who committed the burglaries may be the same persons installing the security systems."

8

Pete and Jenkins went back to the office to finish working on the reports and speak to the captain. He noticed a folder on his desk and opened it. "Look at this!" Pete said.

"What is it?" Jenkins asked.

"It's information from Keith and the tech team from North Miami. It looks like they've identified the bodies from the warehouse kidnapping."

"The one where Elena was involved?"

"Yes. Two of them had prints on the scene of the burglaries where I worked with Elena."

"This is getting stranger by the minute," Jenkins said.

Pete recalled the demon scent was at the downtown burglaries but had been tracked to a card. He didn't recall the scent at the warehouse. "Yes, it is." Then he wondered about the dangers for Elena.

When he was an angel, he could use his abilities to wrap the demon in spiritual chains and hurl him back to the underworld; a different dimension than this one. Without his angelic powers, he could only fight with the armor of

God. Then Luke came to mind. Luke had been tracking the Nephilim to see if she was good or evil. Maybe the demon was doing the same thing. If the demon could convince Alona to join him, he would be extremely powerful.

Jenkins stood. "The captain is here. Let's go."

Elena had been at the station for an hour, working on reports about her kidnapping from the day before. She had a gut feeling that it was only about Alona, and she and Teresa just happened to be there. Her information could help the North Miami detectives working on the investigation. She would have to fill the captain in on what had happened, since she couldn't reach him the day before. She also had to set up an appointment to have the surveillance equipment installed for the shop downtown.

Then she thought about showing the rap sheets to Luke. He would be able to see if the criminals were involved while installing the equipment. Somehow, she would have to patrol the area to be ready to arrest them when Luke identifies them.

She dialed the number for the North Miami detective she had spoken to, hoping to get an update on the identification of the bodies, but the number went to voicemail. She left a message. Maybe he was on a stakeout. Then she dialed the number for the security company.

"Mrs. Cummings, we've had a few people call out sick this week. I'm afraid we won't be able to set up an appointment until next week."

"Next week?" That was cutting it close. "All right, if I have no choice, let's make it for next Wednesday."

Now what could she do? She had to get some kind of

equipment in the shop to make it look like a shop. She thought for a few minutes and realized she could probably rent something for a week. She typed in the name of one company and scrolled through their offerings online. After a while, she searched several companies, but only found furniture. How would she get retail equipment for rent? She could always start with a desk and chair and make it look like she was setting up a business.

She started another search for retail equipment. The more she looked, the more she realized she would have to buy more and more things to make it look like a real shop. Then Catalina's suggestion came to mind. *Why not start a private investigation company?* She finally ordered a desk and chair. It would be delivered on Friday. She would also need a computer, but since she was spending her own money, she would go shopping for one in person. Now was as good a time as any. Before she got out the door, someone stopped her in the hall.

"Did you hear the news?"

"What news?"

"There was a raid on some businesses in North Miami this morning. It ended up in a shoot-out."

Her heart skipped a beat. "Oh, my God!" *'Pete! Are you okay? Speak to me.'*

'Hey babe. I'm good. We busted a drug ring at a business in North Miami. I'll talk to you later.'

That sounded like Pete, but he sounded off, like he was slurring his words. She turned around and headed to the captain's office.

"What happened in North Miami?"

"It was successful for the most part. We busted all three businesses and arrested the owners and managers."

"But?"

"North Miami had a fatality and we had two injuries."

"Who was it?"

"Cummings and Jenkins."

"Where are they?"

"Jackson Memorial."

She turned and ran out the door. She rushed to her car and climbed inside. "Oh God! Please heal both Pete and Jenkins!" She drove as fast as she could to get there, praying all the way.

Once she found her way inside the hospital, she stopped at the nurse's station in the emergency room. "I'm looking for the two detectives that were injured this morning," she said.

The nurse directed her to the waiting room where Elena paced for thirty minutes until someone came out. The surgery nurse spoke to the woman at the nurse's station, then went back inside the operating room.

"Can I see my husband?"

"I'm sorry, the doctor is in surgery right now," the nurse answered.

Elena continued to pace until she realized she hadn't told her family. She sat down and made a few calls. Finally, she went back to the nurse's station.

"Can you tell me anything? Who is in surgery? How bad is it?"

"I'm sorry. When they are finished, they will let me know."

She continued to pace while speaking telepathically to Pete. '*Pete, talk to me. I love you.*'

Finally, another nurse came out and spoke to the nurse at the station. Elena walked toward them. "I need to know if my husband is okay."

"Which one is your husband?" the surgery nurse asked.

"Pete Cummings, and I also want to know about his partner, Jenkins."

"Jenkins is in surgery now for a bullet wound. Cummings is in recovery. I'll come and get you when you can see him."

Elena continued to pray for Pete's healing while she paced. Pete must be unconscious and that's why he hadn't responded. She scrolled through her phone for news feeds to see if she could piece together what happened.

After thirty minutes, the surgery nurse came and spoke to her. "You can see him now. He's in recovery." She led her to the room.

"Pete!" she rushed to his bedside. His chest was bare and his right shoulder was bandaged. Not good. Pete turned his head toward her and blinked a few times before opening his eyes. She stood on his left side. His arm reached out around her waist and squeezed her tight.

"Babe, I'm sorry."

She leaned down and kissed him on the lips. "What are you sorry for?"

"For all this. I couldn't tell you what was going down because it happened so fast. I'll have to tell you about it later. Right now, I can't think straight."

She kissed him again and he returned the kiss with a little more passion. "We'll talk later."

A nurse walked in to check his vitals again. "How's Jenkins?" Pete asked.

"He's out of surgery and in recovery right now."

"Can we see him?" Elena asked.

"There are two gentlemen in there now," the nurse responded.

"Must be Heins and Struber," Pete said.

"I will go check," Elena said. "Be right back."

She found the room. "Excuse me, are you two Heins and Struber?"

"Yes," one of them answered. She walked up to the bed.

"Are you Romero?" one of them asked.

"Cummings. I'm checking on Jenkins for Pete. Are you okay? How are you feeling?"

"I've felt much better. This is going to put a damper on our investigation," Jenkins said.

"Actually, the raid was a success," Struber said. "We arrested everyone at the downtown business and closed it down, without gunfire."

"Yeah, and the South Miami business is done as well. We had no problem there," Heins said.

"So, it was just us that had the shoot-out?" Jenkins asked.

"Apparently," Struber said.

"So, what happened?" Elena asked.

"A North Miami detective went down but so did three of the business people." Heins said.

"Only Jenkins and Cummings were injured," Struber added.

"You know, it was like they were expecting us. Before we even got to the doors, they opened fire on us. Otherwise, how would they know why we were there?"

Elena's heart skipped a beat.

"Where's Cummings?" Jenkins asked.

"Next door. Where were you shot?" she asked.

"My leg. I'll be out of commission for six to eight weeks," Jenkins said.

"I guess you'll be doing all the paperwork, then," Heins said.

"Yeah, right."

"How's Cummings?" Struber asked.

"Looks like a shoulder wound, but I haven't talked to the

doctor yet," she said. "I'm glad you're all right. I'll let Pete know." She left to get back to Pete.

After she spent a few more minutes with Pete, the doctor came in.

"When can he come home, doctor?"

"Well, he needs to stay here tonight for observation, but he possibly can go home tomorrow. I'll have the nurse go over the steps for changing the bandages. And I'll give you a sheet of exercises for him to do until I check him again."

"How bad was it, doctor?" Pete asked.

"The bullet just missed the brachial artery but tore up the muscle on its way out. You were damn lucky it didn't hit the bone. It took a long time to sew you back together. I recommend you stay at least a couple days to make sure there is no more bleeding."

Pete squeezed her hand as the doctor spoke. "What about my partner, Jenkins? Can he go home today?"

"No. I've spoken to him and the two gentlemen that were visiting him. They will take him home tomorrow. One of them volunteered to stay with him a few days to help him out."

After the doctor left, Elena caressed Pete's cheek. "I'll stay with you tonight." She stood beside the bed.

Pete brought her hand to his lips and kissed it. "Elena, two of the bodies from your abduction to the warehouse battle matched the prints from the robberies."

"I knew it! That's why the security company wouldn't let me make an appointment this week. They lost their crew."

"What are you up to?"

"I ordered a desk and chair for the shop downtown and then called to make an appointment to get the security company to install the equipment. But they don't want anyone to see them install it."

"That's weird."

"Yes, but I got Luke to agree to help me when they show up. He will watch them and report anything he sees to me."

"And you are going to be home when this happens?"

"Of course not! I'll be driving around the neighborhood or parked down the street. I want to know why they are so secretive and to identify them if they are the same people who robbed the businesses."

He rubbed her arm. "I want to be there with you."

"I want you there, too. You know, it's hard to pretend to be running a business while working an investigation. It's like I'm trying to split my brain between analytical thinking and creative thinking." She pulled a chair close to the bed. "I need to order a laptop since I didn't get to the store today."

She searched her phone for different laptops and showed them to Pete before ordering one.

"What kind of business are you setting up?" Pete asked.

"I thought a retail shop would work, but it would cost too much to set up even for a couple weeks."

"Maybe you won't need to actually set one up."

"What do you mean?"

"Just do what you're doing. The desk and chair will be enough. And since you're getting a laptop, do you have internet there?"

"I don't know. I guess I could use my phone as a hot spot for now."

"Good idea. The main thing you're doing is trying to catch the burglars installing security equipment, right?"

"See, that's why I like working with you. You help me figure things out."

Elena pulled up the news feeds for Pete to look at so he would know what had transpired after he was injured. She sat with him until late afternoon when she got hungry. She headed down to the cafeteria to find something to eat and call her family. She filled her mother in on Pete's condition.

Angelina mentioned the reception that she and Catalina were planning for the whole family. "It will be in four weeks on our regular get-together," Angelina said.

"At Mom's house?"

"No, we'll have it at the park down the street from her house. I've already reserved it. Be sure to tell Pete."

"Oh, I will."

"Elena, will Pete be able to go back to work?"

"I don't see why not."

"Won't it affect his shooting arm?"

"I don't know. He's got a doctor's appointment next week. We can find out then." It had never dawned on her that his wound would affect his future, but she had seen it happen to others in the department.

She gathered the sandwiches, drinks, and chips for her and Pete and headed back to his room. When she arrived at the room, the nurse was taking his vitals again.

"Is he still good?" she asked.

"Yes, he's fine." The nurse glanced at Pete. "You should be able to go home in a couple of days. In the morning, we will check your wound and change the bandages." The nurse turned back to Elena. "The morning nurse will show you how to do that for when you go home, and she'll go over some other things with you. And be sure he reports to the doctor next week for his follow-up." The nurse handed her two cards. "This is the doctor's number and your appointment time. The other is a number you can call if you have questions for the nurse."

"Thank you."

After the nurse left, Elena shared the food with Pete. He

was hungry because he ate the sandwich quickly and gulped down the water.

"Pete, have you tried healing yourself?"

He stiffened. "I hadn't even thought to do that."

"Well, I've been praying for you."

He motioned for her to come close, so she did. He took her hand in his, closed his eyes and prayed. After a couple minutes, he opened his eyes.

"How do you feel?" she asked.

"Much better. Tomorrow, we'll see the evidence."

"Were you wearing the armor of God?"

"I had it on the other day, but I don't remember if I had it on this morning."

Someone came in with the evening meal and Pete ate all of that and requested more water and ice. It was funny watching him try to eat left-handed, but he got the hang of it soon enough.

She moved his tray and water away from the bed then kicked her shoes off. She climbed into bed beside him and curled up against his good arm and shoulder. It was cramped in the single hospital bed, but more comfortable than the chair. She dozed off, but her sleep didn't last long. The night nurse came in to get Pete's vitals again and made her move off the bed.

"Hon, why don't you go on home so you both can get some sleep," the nurse said.

"I don't want to leave my husband."

"I'm giving him some meds so he can sleep."

Pete pulled her close and kissed her. "Come and get me out of here first thing in the morning," Pete whispered.

"Okay," she whispered back. Elena left reluctantly and headed to her car. Before driving off, she called her mother. "Pete's fine, but they suggested I leave so we both can sleep."

"Well, that makes sense," her mother said.

"I miss him at night."

"Oh, I know you do. I did, too, when they changed our schedules. We worked it out, though. We eventually got the same days off and then the same hours, but it took a while. I'll pray for you to be on the same schedule," her mother said.

"Thanks, Mom." Elena started up her car and headed home. By the time she pulled into the driveway, she had a strange feeling come over her. She immediately put on the armor of God. Why hadn't she done that earlier when she spoke to Pete about it?

She locked her car and headed to the front door, but an awful smell hit her. It was stronger the closer she moved to the door, like a sewer had leaked. Then the strange feeling came back. She glanced around. Something, maybe Lia, was telling her to get out of there. She rushed back to her car and fumbled with the key. She realized her hand was shaking while trying to unlock her old Mustang. If only she had a button to push to unlock her door, like Pete had on his truck.

Finally, she got the door open and climbed inside. She immediately locked her door and stuck the key in the ignition. It fired right up. She threw the gear shift in reverse and floored it. She got out on the road and put the gear in drive and sped off. She never drove this recklessly, but she had to get out of there. She drove straight to the only other place where she felt safe, her mother's house, praying all the way.

9

———————

"Elena! What are you doing here?" her father asked. "Come in, come in."

"Something or someone was at my house. I just couldn't go in there." She moved into the entryway.

"Oh, Elena! You look like you've seen a ghost," her mother said. She reached for Elena's arm and walked her into the living room.

"Worse than that," she said. "It smelled like a sewer erupted at my door, but I think it was a demon."

"A demon?" her mother asked.

"Yes, we're dealing with a demon. I think he was responsible for Pete's injury as well as Jenkins, and the death of the detective from North Miami."

Her father brought a couple beers into the living room. "Here, you need this. Now talk."

She explained in more detail everything that had been going on with her case and Pete's case. She mentioned the abduction at the warehouse.

"What? Why didn't you tell us?" her mother asked.

"So much has happened so quickly, I just forgot."

"Don't let that happen again, Elena. We're family. We need to know these things," her father said.

She finished filling them in and finally went to bed. The beer helped her relax a bit and she was able to doze off soon enough.

The next morning, Elena bolted from her bed. She had to tell Pete about last night. Had she imagined everything?

'No. It was the demon searching for you,' she heard in her head.

'Lia, is that you?' she asked telepathically.

'Yes.'

After sharing breakfast with her parents, her father volunteered to go with her to help get Pete home and pick up his truck.

There was an awkward silence as they drove to the hospital. Once she was there, the nurses did not want to release Pete due to the severity of his injury.

"Let's check it, while you show me how to change the bandages," she suggested.

"The doctor wants him to stay for a couple days," the nurse said.

"Well, if all he is going to do is sleep, he can do that at home with me taking care of him. I will give him more attention than you have time for here."

"We're better trained in this case," the nurse said.

"I've had extensive first aid training as well as some EMT training in my line of duty, so I think I can handle it," Elena said.

The nurse finally acquiesced and showed Elena how to change the bandages. She was slightly surprised to see there was no mark on the front of his shoulder. "I can't believe it," she said.

"What is it?" Pete asked.

"There's no scar or hole or stitches," the nurse said.

"He's been healed," Elena said.

Rafael looked over their shoulders. The nurse checked the back of his shoulder where the doctor said there was more damage. "Oh, my! There's nothing here either," she said.

"I guess we won't need the bandages or the sling," Elena said.

"I think I'll keep the sling for a souvenir," Pete said.

Elena gathered his things together. "You two wait here while I fill out those forms," she said.

She headed back with the nurse and signed the forms to release Pete. By the time she finished, a nurse wheeled Pete out into the hall with Rafael following, carrying Pete's things. Pete had changed into the clothes he wore when he was shot. She realized she had forgotten to bring him a change of clothes. Everything was covered in blood.

"I'm so sorry, Pete. I didn't bring you anything to change into."

"I'm good, Elena. Nothing to worry about."

When they got to the door, Elena rushed out to the parking lot to retrieve her car. She pulled up to where Pete, Rafael and the nurse waited. Pete got into the passenger side, while her father moved her seat and told her he was driving.

"This is not how I pictured this in my mind," she said.

"There's not enough leg room for me or Pete in your back seat," her father said. She reluctantly climbed in and realized how true that statement was when her father pushed her driver seat further back into her knees.

"Where's your truck?" Rafael asked Pete.

"North Miami, at the scene of the crime." Pete said.

Her father drove in that direction and Pete gave him the address.

"Last night, I think I encountered the demon," she said.

Pete turned toward her. "What did you say?"

She explained what had happened with the intense smell and the feeling she had to get out of there.

"That smell was definitely a demon. That's the smell that was on that card we threw away and in each of those businesses we investigated. I'm glad you listened to Lia," Pete said.

"Who is Lia?" her father asked.

"Her Guardian Angel," Pete said.

Rafael glanced at Pete. "Are you serious?"

"Yes, sir. When I started working with Elena, I was still an angel. I spoke to Lia, and she spoke to me. I could see her. I gave that gift to Elena."

"I haven't seen Lia, but now I can hear her more clearly. I only saw shadows at our house."

"Even if the demon wasn't there, his stench would remain for a while," Pete said.

"I might have just missed him," she said.

"I'm glad you did," Pete said.

"Have you put on your armor today?" she asked.

"No."

"Let's do it, now," she said. She silently uttered the prayer from Ephesians 6:10–17, while going through the motions of putting on the armor.

"What are you two talking about?" Rafael asked.

"We put on the armor of God every day for protection," Pete said.

"And that really works?" Rafael asked.

"Yes, it does," Elena said.

By the time they reached the business, it was almost lunchtime. Elena and her father exited the Mustang. She handed her father the keys to Pete's truck. "Be careful, Dad. See you at my house."

"Let him take it home until I can drive again," Pete said.

"I thought you were healed," Elena said.

"I am, but they gave me some medication this morning that's making me a little dizzy," Pete said.

"Are you sure?" Rafael asked.

"I trust you," Pete said.

Elena kissed her father on the cheek and climbed back into the front seat where she belonged. It took a few minutes to adjust her seat. "I don't like riding as a passenger in my own car." She waited to make sure her father was able to drive Pete's truck since it was a lot newer than his own truck with all the extra tech on it. She glanced around the area. The business was cordoned off, with guards at the door.

"What did the captain say about you taking off work?" Pete asked.

She watched her father drive off and then followed behind him. "I didn't tell him. I just did it. I couldn't think straight with you in the hospital. Besides, he knew where you were. He should have expected me to be with you."

Pete took her hand while she drove. "I missed you last night."

"I missed you, too." She drove a while then pulled into a fast-food restaurant when she heard Pete's stomach growl. "Can you hold on until we get home? We're almost there."

Pete was dozing off as they pulled into the driveway. She helped him get out of the car.

"I think I'll take a nap before I eat," Pete said.

"What did they give you this morning?"

"I don't know. There are some pills in my bag." Pete glanced around while she unlocked the door. "I don't smell anything," he said.

She sniffed the air. "I don't either, so that's good."

Pete stumbled in the house and she guided him to the bedroom. "Are you going to be okay?" she asked.

"Yeah, I'm just real tired. I guess those pills kicked in while we drove home." He sat on the edge of the bed. She pulled his shoes off and helped him lie back on the pillows.

"Are you comfortable?"

"Yes." In a blink of an eye, he was out.

Elena finished getting his things in the house and pulled out some clean clothes for when he woke up. Then she sat down and ate her sandwich. She didn't have much to do today at the office and her investigation was at a standstill until the security company could install the equipment. She decided to call the captain and let him know where she was in the investigation and that she was taking time off to help Pete.

After a short call, the captain wasn't too happy about three people being out of work, but he owed her some time off since she worked overtime during the cruise investigation in Puerto Rico, where she and Pete tied the knot. The thought made her smile.

After an hour or so, Pete awoke hungry. She heated up his sandwich and sat with him while he ate.

"Well, you've gotten your appetite back," she said.

"I don't think I ever lost it."

"You're right."

"I think I'll take a shower and maybe I'll feel normal again."

"As if you ever were normal," she laughed.

"And what does that mean?"

She stood up and reached her hands to caress his face. "It means you've always been special to me. You're stronger, smarter, and braver than any other man I know, so that makes you above normal."

He wrapped his arms around her and kissed her passionately. She returned the kiss and didn't want to let go.

"Let me get this grime off me and we'll continue this after I shower."

"It's a deal," she said. She watched him take the clothes off the bed and walk into the bathroom. She kicked off her shoes and sat back on the bed. She pulled her book off the nightstand, opened it up where she left off and started reading.

A few minutes later, Pete came into the room, wearing just his jeans. "I want you to check my shoulder again," he said.

"Sure. Does it hurt?"

"No. I rotated my shoulder a few times. It feels great. I just want to make sure there aren't any scars since I can't see the back of my shoulder."

"I got you. I have a better idea." She got up and retrieved a mirror from the bathroom and showed him where to stand so he could see the back of his shoulder with the help of an extra mirror.

"Perfect. No scars," he said.

She kissed the back of his shoulder where the bullet had left his body. "Hmm. You taste good there, too."

"What are you doing?"

"I'm enjoying this perfect shoulder," she said. Then she kissed the front of his shoulder, then his chest.

He lifted her chin and kissed her lips. Then he kissed her neck and worked his way down to her chest before stopping. He scooped her up in his arms and carried her to the bed. He blinked off their clothes and continued kissing her all over.

"Hmm, I really missed this," she said.

They continued kissing and licking each other until their passions got the best of them and they came together in a heated climax.

"I don't want to let you go," she said. She clung to him as he turned over on his back.

"Don't, then." He wrapped his arms around her and just held her against his naked flesh.

"I thank God you are alive," she whispered.

"Me, too."

"I told the captain I would be out with you while you recuperate," she said.

"You didn't tell him I was healed?"

"No and he didn't ask."

"I'll help you with your investigation until I have to return to work."

"Thank you." She ran her fingers across his chest. "Since you prayed for a healing for Jenkins, do you think he's good now, too?"

"I'm sure he is, but he doesn't realize it yet. We'll pay him a visit this week."

After spending the afternoon cuddling, Elena and Pete discussed their cases. "I can see how these are tied together since the abductions," Elena said. "If we can identify the remaining criminals, we can take down that security company as well."

"Your appointment is for next Wednesday?" Pete asked.

"Yes."

"Well, I'm off that day, so I'll go with you."

Elena's phone rang. It was her father's ring tone.

"Hey, Dad. Did you make it home okay?"

"Yes, but I have some bad news."

Elena sat up. "What is it?" She hit the speaker button so Pete could hear.

"Remember when I told you I was thinking of starting a charter boat business?"

"Yes. You were going to hire Jimmy, right?"

"Yes. And Jimmy got Adriana to agree to let us moor the boat at her new bar and grill."

"Great. So, what's the bad news?"

Pete moved closer to her.

"Jimmy and Adriana are missing. Neither of them is answering their phone. Jimmy called me Saturday night with the news about mooring the boat. I tried calling him on Sunday with no luck. I've tried again on Monday and today, but he's still not answering the phone. It goes to voicemail. My brother, Jaime, called me this morning and said he hasn't heard from either one of them since Saturday."

"Oh, my God! What do you need me to do?"

"Jaime already alerted the authorities in the Keys. I need you to call all your mutual friends and see if they've heard from them or know anything about their whereabouts."

"Sure, Dad. I'll do that now."

"Your mother and I are heading to the Keys in the morning to help with the search."

"We'll go with you," Pete said.

"I appreciate that. If we have to search every Key, we will. I'm bringing the boat trailer in case we need it," Rafael said.

Elena went through her contact list and called everyone she could think of who knew her family. She made calls for hours. If no one answered, she left a message. When her phone battery went to red, she plugged it into the charger, then headed to the bathroom to take a shower. When she finished, she found Pete packing some clothes.

"I found this suitcase in the closet. I hope you don't mind?"

"Of course not. What's mine is yours." She took some clothes out of the dresser and packed along with Pete. She pulled out a large toiletry bag and filled it with supplies.

"I'll call the captain in the morning and let him know what we're up to." It had been a long day and she and Pete went to bed when they had everything packed and ready.

The next morning, Elena texted her father to wait on her and Pete. Then she called the captain and let him know she had a family emergency and would be out of town for a few days while Pete was healing.

"How are you feeling?" Pete asked, rubbing her back.

"A little anxious, but I'm believing they are both fine."

"I believe it, too. I'll get a better feel for the situation by being there."

"I'll drive while you call Jenkins," she said. "I see you're wearing your arm brace. Is your shoulder bothering you?"

"No. I don't want to run into anyone we know at the department. This is merely a precaution."

"Good." They loaded the car and packed something to eat on the way to the Keys. Once they were on the road, Pete punched in Jenkins' number.

"Hello Jenkins, it's me, Cummings. How are you feeling today?"

"I feel so much better now that I'm home. How about you?" Jenkins asked.

"I'm healed. I prayed for your healing as well. In fact, I threw away all those pills. I don't need them."

"Are you kidding? Those things weren't cheap."

"You don't need yours anymore either, so stop taking them."

"I don't know about that."

"Try not taking them today and see how you feel. Can you wriggle your toes?"

"Yes. Wow."

"Any pain?"

"No. Hey, that's incredible. They don't look swollen anymore either."

Pete explained about the family emergency. "I'll call you when we get back and I'll come and check on you."

"Hey, Cummings, when you said you were healed, what did you mean by that?"

"I can use my arm like nothing ever happened to it. There's no scar or any mark that showed I was even injured."

"Is that one of your gifts?"

"Yes."

When Pete hung up, Elena pulled into her parents' driveway, beside Pete's truck.

"Let's take my truck," he said.

"Is it my driving?"

"No, babe, the truck is more comfortable and has GPS."

"Yeah, you're right."

Pete removed their things from the car and put them in the cab of the truck, while wearing his arm sling.

Elena knocked on the door and her father answered. She hugged him. "How are Tio and Tia doing this morning?"

"Jaime and Maria are upset, but they are trying to keep it together. Come in."

Elena entered and Pete followed behind her.

"How's your shoulder, Pete? Should you be out like this?" Rafael asked.

"It's good as new after being healed. I'm just wearing this in case we see anyone from the

department." Pete took off the sling and demonstrated.

Mama walked into the room. "I just booked rooms at a hotel in Marathon. I'm ready." She set her suitcase down for dad to pack in his truck.

"Who else is going?" Elena asked.

"Just us. I told the girls I couldn't babysit, so they are staying home with the kids so we can help with the search. They may join us on the weekend if we're still there," her mother said.

Rafael and Liz got into Rafael's truck after he attached the trailer. Elena moved her car into their garage after her father pulled the truck out. Then she joined Pete in his truck, and they followed her parents down the road.

10

———

A couple hours later, Elena and Pete pulled into the hotel parking lot in Marathon behind her parents. There, they met up with her Tio Jaime and Tia Maria.

"I called the police as well as the Coast Guard. I last heard from Jimmy late Saturday night. He said he was at the Toasted Coconut and helped Adriana with her customers," Tio Jaime said.

"I talked with him as well and he said he may sleep over at Adriana's apartment since it was so late," Tia Maria said.

"I talked to him Saturday, too, when he told me Adriana said we could moor the boat at her dock," Rafael said.

"Is Jimmy in the habit of calling you all a lot?" Pete asked.

"Yes. We keep in touch all the time since he was living with us again," Tia Maria said.

"Again?" Elena asked.

"He broke up with his girlfriend. They had been living together in an apartment in Miami. He was looking for a new place to live, when he started working for Rafael," Tio Jaime said.

"Okay, that's a start," Pete said.

"Did you tell the police all of this?" Elena asked.

"No, just that we hadn't heard from him since Saturday," Tio Jaime said.

"Since he called you a lot, that would have been good to know that you hadn't heard anything from him since then, especially since it's now Wednesday," Pete said.

"Jimmy said he moored the boat at Adriana's place. We can take the boat and do some searching ourselves," Rafael said.

"Here are some pictures of the two of them," Tia Maria said. She showed them to Pete first since he didn't know either of them.

Elena glanced over his arm to see if they had changed since the last time she had seen them. Both Jimmy and Adriana sported good tans and looked like siblings with their dark brown hair and brown eyes. It was when they were both in their military uniforms.

"We are meeting with the police at 1:00 p.m. to show them the pictures," Tia Maria said.

"Be sure and let them know everything you just told us. It would be helpful in their investigation," Elena said.

"While you are doing that, we will head down to Coconut Key and pick up the boat. We will meet here later this afternoon," Rafael said.

Elena's parents got into their truck and pulled the boat trailer down to Coconut Key. Pete and Elena climbed into Pete's truck and followed them. By the time they made it to the Toasted Coconut Bar and Grill, the police were already there, and the place was cordoned off.

"We found no suspicious entry," an officer told her

father. "They are finding fingerprints now so the place will remain cordoned off until they've finished."

Elena introduced herself and Pete and showed them both their badges. "We'd like to help in any way we can. What can we do that won't interfere with your investigation?" she asked.

"Talk to their friends and see what they know," the officer said.

"Can we look around at the dock?" Pete asked.

"Sure. I think they've already gotten prints from the boat," the officer said. Pete escorted Elena to the dock.

"This is a nice place," Elena said. "Adriana called it her paradise."

Pete stood a few feet away from the boat, his arms crossed.

"Do you feel anything strange about this?" Elena asked.

"No and I don't sense anything dangerous or evil."

"What about Lia?" Elena asked. "Can she speak to their Guardian Angels?"

"That's a great idea," Pete said. He closed his eyes and raised his arms as in an uplifting prayer. About that time, Rafael and Liz came from the front side of the Grill toward the dock.

"The police said I can take the boat," Rafael said.

"How will you get it out of the water?" Elena asked.

"There's a small ramp over on Duck Key. I'll see if they will let me use it. In the meantime, I could use some extra eyes on the water."

"What about the Coast Guard?" she asked.

"They are checking the Gulf side. I thought we could start around here and go toward the Atlantic side."

"Let us know," Elena said. She watched her father walk

back around the front of the Grill. Her mother stayed with them.

After a few minutes, her father called Pete on his phone.

"Sure, I'll be right there," Pete said.

"I'm going to pick up your father after he parks his truck on Duck Key, then we'll be back."

Elena touched his arm. "I need a hug," she said. She wrapped her arms around Pete and he hugged her back, tight. Then he gave her a kiss. "Hmm, that helps a lot. I feel much better." She walked to the edge of the pier and watched Pete walk away. Then she sat down beside her mother, dangling her legs over the water.

"I can see why Adriana thought this was paradise," she said.

"Yes?"

"Yes, it makes me smile. It's beautiful here."

"I feel so helpless in this situation," her mother said.

"I hope they are both enjoying the day and just let the time get away from them," Elena said.

"Me, too, but it's two days since her business was supposed to be opened. Adriana is a responsible young woman. This isn't like her."

Elena hugged her mother.

"I don't know how I would handle this if it was one of you girls."

"You're much stronger than Tia Maria. I think you would be fine," Elena said.

Liz patted Elena's hand.

After about thirty minutes, Pete came back with her father. "We're ready, if you two are," Rafael said.

Elena helped her mother up off the pier and the four of them got into the boat. It started up just fine. Her father circled Coconut Key and then Duck Key. Then he headed toward the Atlantic, hugging the coastline as much as possible. Liz, Rafael, Elena and Pete all watched in different directions, looking for anything unusual. After a couple hours, Rafael headed back but further out as they checked for signs of Adriana and Jimmy. Instead of pulling up to Adriana's dock, Rafael drove the boat to Duck Key and up to the ramp. Pete got out and helped Elena out, then her mother. Pete climbed into Rafael's truck and backed the trailer onto the ramp and in the water, where Rafael drove the boat onto the trailer. It took a few more minutes before the boat was hooked up and Rafael and Liz headed back to the hotel in Marathon. Pete and Elena followed in Pete's truck.

"I don't have the feeling that Adriana and Jimmy are in the ocean," Pete said.

"Have you heard from Lia?" Elena asked.

"Not yet."

"Why do you have that feeling?" she asked.

"When we were on the dock, I felt the frequency was a little higher in one spot. It was more of a pleasant feeling and not anything sinister."

"Frequency?"

"Yes, remember? All living things vibrate at different frequencies. When I was an angel, I vibrated at a higher frequency and was able to do more things than now. Humans vibrate at a lower frequency."

"So, you lowered your frequency to be human?"

"Pretty much."

"If you can lower your frequency, can you also raise it?"

"That's a good question. You can start by meditating."

"Really? I wish I had time for that."

"You make time. Also, being grateful is another way."

"Grateful?"

"Yes, and love toward others as well as being generous."

"It sounds too easy."

"It's not that easy, really. Especially since we are dealing with criminals and the dregs of society. Then there is forgiveness and thinking positive thoughts."

"Is this something we can do together?"

"Certainly. We can start when we get home, but we need to think positive thoughts now to help your aunt and uncle get through this."

"Yes. Positive thoughts. I believe we will find both of them and they will be perfectly fine and happy."

"There you go. That's a start."

After a while, they arrived at the hotel. Elena and Pete headed to their room.

"I think I'll shower to get this salt spray off me," she said.

Pete lay on the bed, resting, until Elena's phone rang. Pete glanced at the ID. It was her father, so Pete answered.

"Hello, this is Pete, Elena's in the shower."

"We'll meet you in the lobby in an hour to get something to eat," Rafael said.

"That's fine. See you then." He ended the call.

When Elena was finished, he filled her in and headed to the shower. By the time he was ready, so was Elena.

"Another thing that will raise your frequency is eating more fruits and vegetables," he said.

"Got it, but does that mean I have to eat less meat?"

"Yes, it does." Pete held the door for her.

"That's going to be hard," she said. They walked toward the elevator.

"We'll work on that together," he said. Pete pushed the button for the elevator.

As the door opened, Elena wrapped her arm through Pete's and stepped inside. "I think eating less meat is the hardest thing I'll have to do," she said.

"Well, consuming less alcohol is another one, and I've grown fond of beer."

"What else?" she asked.

"Listening to positive music or reading uplifting books, or watching uplifting movies is good," he said.

Elena clung to Pete as they walked to the lobby. He enjoyed her closeness.

Both her parents and Tia Maria and Tio Jaime were in the lobby, waiting for them. They all walked a short distance to a local restaurant to eat. Once inside, it wasn't long before they were seated.

"The police are doing all they can, but it feels as if they could do more," Maria said.

"They are going by the evidence and whatever clues they can find," Elena said.

"Did you tell them everything you knew about them and your last conversation," Pete asked.

"Yes, but I don't think it was helpful," Jaime said.

"Unless we question everyone who was there, we can only guess at what happened," Pete said.

"That's it!" Elena said. She sat up. "Maybe you could put out a PSA, you know, a public service announcement in the local papers asking for information on the last known whereabouts of Jimmy and Adriana, and for the patrons of the Toasted Coconut Bar and Grill to come forward with any information."

"I think that's a good idea," Jaime said. "I'll work on that tomorrow."

"Tomorrow, I'd like to drive the boat from here to Coconut Key and see if we find anything," Rafael said.

"Jaime and I will drive from here to Key West by car and see if we discover anything," Maria said.

"What about you, two?" Liz asked Elena.

Pete glanced at Elena and shrugged. "We're open. We can help you search by boat, if you want?" Elena said.

"Sure, that's fine with me," he said.

The next day, Rafael Romero found a place to launch his boat. This time, he brought food and drinks and two coolers with plenty of ice. The trip took hours to go from the Atlantic side to Coconut Key. The plan was to return up the Gulf side.

When they arrived at Coconut Key, Adriana's place was still cordoned off. "I think we should fish around the Key for a while," Rafael said.

"Fish? I thought we were searching for Adriana and Jimmy?" Elena asked.

"You never know what you'll find when you go fishing," Rafael said. He cut the engine and picked up a fishing pole stashed along the inside of the boat. Rafael opened a small cooler and pulled out some live bait and baited a hook. He then handed the pole to Pete. "Here, try this," Rafael said.

"I've never been fishing," Pete said.

"I'll show you. It's easy," Rafael said. He demonstrated how to cast the line and then handed the pole to Pete. "You don't set the hook initially, but wait until you feel something on the line, then set it." Rafael picked up another pole and began fishing with Pete.

"Did you bring enough poles for me and Mama?" Elena asked.

"I didn't think you'd want to fish," Rafael said.

"What did you think Mama and I were going to do?"

"You can watch," Rafael said.

Pete hid a smile.

"Do I look like the kind of woman who likes to sit and watch?" Her fisted hands were on her hips.

"No, I guess not," her father said.

She turned and sat next to her mother on a bench seat, her arms crossed.

"I brought a couple of books," her mother said. Liz pulled a romance novel out of her beach bag.

"If I had known he was going to fish, I would have been prepared to fish," she said.

"Here, you can read this one," Her mother handed her a book.

Elena flipped the book over. It was a cozy mystery by Kimberley O'Malley, "A Dress to Die For." "Hmm, this looks interesting." She opened the book and started reading. The fact that she had time to read reminded her of the time before she met Pete. She had more time alone and reading filled the void. Until their schedules were changed, she had no time to read. But now that they were adjusting to the different schedules, she found that time again.

"I got something!" Pete shouted.

"Reel it in, like this," Rafael said. He showed Pete how to do it.

Elena and her mother put their books down to watch the action. Before Pete reeled his fish in all the way, Rafael got a bite. Rafael traded poles with Pete and helped Pete get his fish in the boat with a gaff hook, then got his own fish in the boat.

"That looks like a grouper," Elena said.

"Yes, we got two groupers today. We'll be eating fish for a good while," Rafael said. Rafael put both fish in the live well and then he and Pete continued fishing with some cut bait. After another hour and a couple of big red snappers, Rafael headed back up the Gulf to Marathon.

Elena had gotten almost halfway finished with her book when she had to put it up. The ride back was too choppy to read.

Once they arrived at the marina in Marathon, Rafael showed Pete how to clean the fish, while Elena and her mother went to find a shop to purchase plastic bags for the fish. They put the fish in the second cooler with the ice. Pete and Rafael carried the ice chests to the truck. Once they were back at the hotel, they drained off the excess water and then used the luggage rack to get the two ice chests to the room.

"We'll split the fish when we get home," Rafael said.

"Are we leaving tomorrow?" Elena asked.

"I'm not sure. I'll check with Jaime tonight and see what he thinks."

Once again, everyone met at the small, nearby restaurant.

"The police said the case would remain open and they would continue to follow any leads," Jaime said.

"The PSA has already produced some calls," Maria said.

"What about Adriana's restaurant?" Elena asked.

"We will stay another day and put a sign up that it's closed until further notice," Maria said.

"What have you heard from the Coast Guard?" Pete asked.

"They have been searching with boats and helicopters with no luck. They are calling off the search unless some new evidence shows up," Jaime said.

"Well, we will head back tomorrow, then," Rafael said.

"You call us immediately if anything changes," Liz said.

"Of course," Maria said. She touched Liz' hand.

Elena spent the evening cuddling with Pete and watching a movie.

"Lia just spoke to me," Pete said.

Elena sat up. "Are they all right? Are they safe?"

"Both of them are fine but their return will be later," he said.

"How much later?"

"Maybe years from now."

Elena got up from the bed and paced the floor. "I need to call Tia Maria and Tio Jaime."

"It's late. We'll call them in the morning. There's nothing they can do for Adriana and Jimmy, now, anyway."

She stopped pacing. Pete held his arms out and she went to him. "I'm so glad I found you," she said.

He kissed her sweetly on the lips. But his kiss led to more kisses and caresses until they were both in the throes of extasy.

Elena slept well, knowing she had Pete beside her. But when she woke, she stressed over how she would tell her relatives about Adriana and Jimmy.

"We'll both tell them. They can either accept it or not. If

they accept it, they can move on, knowing the two will return."

"I hope so."

A few minutes later, everything was packed, and they headed down to the lobby to load up the truck.

Tia Maria and Tio Jaime were in the lobby, speaking to her parents.

"We have good news," Pete said.

All eyes were on Pete. He put his hand on Elena's back and glanced at her. "Adriana and Jimmy are fine, but they won't be back for a while," he said.

"How do you know this?" Tia Maria asked.

Elena glanced up at Pete. "Pete has psychic powers," she said.

"A psychic?" Tio Jaime said.

Rafael rubbed his forehead. Liz covered her mouth.

"The truth is, I was once an angel. I still have angelic connections and asked Elena's Guardian Angel to find out what's happened to both of them."

"An angel?" Tia Maria said.

Pete nodded. "Lia didn't say what happened to them except they were both fine. They would return in years."

"Years?" Tia Maria said.

"An angel? You were an angel? What happened? Why are you no longer an angel?" Liz asked.

Elena put her arm through Pete's arm. "I fell in love with your daughter. I couldn't live on Earth and in Heaven, so I chose to be on Earth with Elena."

"I can't believe we are having this conversation," Tio Jaime said.

"Believe it, Jaime. I saw for myself. Just be glad he's in the family. I would rather have angelic friends than demon friends," Rafael said.

"Do you still have your angelic powers?" Liz asked.

"Some of them."

"Okay, let's stop right there. We need to get on the road. Are you coming, Jaime?" Rafael asked.

"I guess we might as well leave today. There's no point in continuing the search. We can contact the bank about the Toasted Coconut and make arrangements with them," Jaime said.

"All right. Come by the house when you get back in town. We'll have fish for supper," Rafael said. He turned and pointed to Pete. "You both will come and have dinner with us and we will split the rest of the fish."

"Yes, sir."

11

———

"I need to check on Jenkins," Pete said. They had just passed the sign that they were in Dade County.

"Sure, we have time," Elena said.

Pete called Jenkins through the truck's voice command.

"Hello?"

"Hey, Jenkins, how are you doing?"

"Pete?"

"Yes. I told you I would call to check on you. Mind if we stop by?"

"We?"

"Elena and I. We're coming back from the Keys. We had a family emergency down there."

"Yeah, right. I bet you went fishing while you were there, too."

"You guessed it. I need your address so we can stop by."

Jenkins gave up his address and Pete put it in the GPS. They arrived within twenty minutes.

Pete knocked at the door, but no one answered. He tried again. A very faint voice called out, "Come in." Pete opened the door and stepped inside. Elena followed behind.

The room was dark where the curtains had been pulled closed. The sun was shining outside, so it took a few minutes to adjust to the darkness.

"Where are you, Jenkins? It's dark in here," Pete said.

"I'm in the back of the house," he called out.

Pete and Elena followed the voice down the hall and found Jenkins in a bedroom on the right.

The bedroom was also dark. Pete flipped on the light. Jenkins sat in a chair near a window. A large, king bed between them and Jenkins.

"It's beautiful outside, why keep it dark in here?" Pete asked.

"I have trouble getting up and down with these damn crutches. I just gave up and left the curtains closed," Jenkins said.

"Remember I told you I prayed for your healing?"

"Yeah, but the doc says I have to wear this cast for six weeks," Jenkins said.

"Haven't you noticed the healing?" Elena asked.

"I noticed the pain has been gone since Pete told me. I quit taking the pills."

"Let's see if we can remove the cast," Pete said.

"The captain is expecting both of us back at work next week on the desk," Jenkins said.

Elena glanced at Pete. He touched her shoulder. "I will be your backup, babe. Don't worry," Pete said.

"What's up?" Jenkins asked.

Elena explained her situation with the security company and Pete explained about the Dark Demon.

"I'll get the boys to help back her up," Jenkins said.

"Good. Now, have you got some scissors?" Pete asked.

"Scissors?"

"Do you want this cast off or not?"

"Check that drawer," Jenkins pointed to his dresser.

Pete found a pair of scissors and used them to cut through the tough cast. When he finished, he handed the scissors back to Jenkins. "You're going to need new scissors," Pete said.

Jenkins stood up and tried out his leg. "Hey, my leg feels great!" He bent to examine the lower portion. "No scars. Wow! Pete, no scars." The two high fived each other.

"Thanks for the healing, man," Jenkins said. "Oh, by the way, we still have to speak to the psychiatrist on Monday."

"What time? I also have a follow-up visit with my doctor next week."

"Ten. I'll text you the address."

"Thanks. See you then."

Pete and Elena headed home. After unpacking, the two spent a couple hours just chilling and being in each other's company.

"I'm going to miss not seeing you every day," she said.

He hugged her to him. "We'll work it out. Let's talk about your cases before heading to your parents' house."

Elena reviewed her findings with Pete until her father texted her about the cookout.

Once they arrived at her parents' house, she realized her sisters were also there. Elena helped her mother in the kitchen, while Pete helped her father with the fish cooker.

"How's your new schedule working out?" Angelina asked.

"We pass each other at the station. I didn't see him much at all when he was on the stakeout," Elena said.

"Mom said you think Adriana and Jimmy are coming back?" Catalina asked.

"Yes. Pete got that information." She stopped herself from saying more. She didn't know if her sisters would believe her if she told them about Pete's past.

Her mother patted her back. "It's okay. They know," she said.

"What's it like being married to an angel?" Catalina asked.

"It's quite nice." She smiled, thinking of her evenings with Pete, in bed.

"Catalina and I have planned your reception party," Angelina said.

"Oh?"

"Yes. I already told you it's in one month, at our next family get together. I'm inviting all the relatives," Angelina said.

"Yes, and we need a list of things you need for the house," Catalina said.

"I've lived alone for years now. I don't think I need anything," Elena said.

"All right, a list of what you *want*, then," Angelina said.

"Okay, okay. When do you need the list?"

"This week," Angelina said.

"Here, take this out to the table," Liz said. She handed Elena and Catalina a bowl of cornbread each.

Before Elena headed back into the kitchen, Angelina came out with a bowl of coleslaw. Then Liz handed Elena a bowl of potato salad.

Pete walked in with Rafael and the two brothers-in-law, Juan and Rick. All of them carried plates of fish. By the time the table was set, the children ran into the dining room.

Angelina and Catalina picked through the fish for the kids, making sure there were no bones. Elena watched Rick do the same with the fish for one of the kids. She pictured herself doing that for her future child.

She enjoyed this visit since she wasn't in the hot seat with her sisters and family. Pete seemed to be getting along with all the men in the family, too. They hung out with the family for a couple hours before leaving, but Elena made sure she helped clean up the mess.

She was grateful for the time she spent with all of them, but her feelings were mixed with sadness at the loss of her two cousins. They had played together as children on many occasions and kept up with each other in high school. Both Adriana and Jimmy were younger than Catalina, so it was like having younger siblings. Not knowing when they would return was hard. She would have to think of them as still being in the military, where she couldn't call them. But at least in the military, she had been able to write to them on occasion.

Elena believed her angel, Lia, told the truth, but she felt something was left out of the translation. Maybe Lia couldn't relay the whole truth, or she didn't know the whole truth herself. She also felt sad, knowing Pete would return to his schedule at work and she would lose her time with him once more.

She relished the chances to express her thoughts on her cases out loud to Pete, which helped her to think things through. Pete usually added some insight to make her thoughts coalesce into solutions.

Pete drove his truck home while she drove her car. She

thought about the security company that would install the equipment on Wednesday. Of course, they had something to hide, otherwise, why be so secretive? But since they lost a whole team of installers/burglars, they had to find someone else to do the job and train them quickly.

Since Alona Gabriel annihilated all those people in the warehouse, she put some bad guys away for good. She would have to touch base with her tomorrow and see what had come of that investigation. She had a lot of loose ends to tie up this week. She hoped that Luke was still able to help her in some way.

The next morning, Pete was up making breakfast, while she dressed for work. She headed toward the kitchen.

"Something sure smells good in here," she said.

Pete cooked eggs while a plate of bacon sat on the counter, next to the stove. "I thought I'd fix us something to eat, while I still had time with you," Pete said.

She walked up behind him and wrapped her arms around his waist. "I'm going to miss this."

She heard him move the pan and then he turned around to hold her. He held her tightly to him. "We will work this out somehow. I'm hoping I'll be back home after visiting the psychiatrist and then the doctor."

"Two in one day? You'll need to see how much sick leave you have left," she said.

"I'll cook supper, so don't be late," Pete said.

They sat together and ate breakfast.

"You know, being late or early depends on the bad guys," she said.

"Make sure the bad guys are taken care of by five o'clock."

"Yes, sir." She saluted him.

After breakfast, the good-bye kiss became a little steamy. "You need to go before I blink your clothes off right here in the living room."

She glanced down at his erection and grabbed her purse and keys on the way out the door. She had been tempted to provoke him, but she had already taken extra time off for her family emergency. She had to update the captain on her progress with the cases, along with writing up the reports.

By the time she arrived at the station, a couple people asked her if she was all right. They had heard she had an emergency but didn't know what kind. She briefly mentioned her missing cousins and headed for her desk. Before she got there, another person asked her about Pete and Jenkins.

Rather than make something up, she told the truth. "They are both doing much better, thanks." She set her things down and picked her files up off the desk. She glanced through each folder and made notes of things to follow up on when her phone rang. It was the captain and he wanted to see her.

She went inside his office and updated him the best she could without the reports.

"I want those reports by the end of the day, Romero."

"It's Cummings, sir."

"I found a candidate for you to train as a partner."

"Okay. Who is it?"

"Someone from west Florida. Pensacola, to be exact. He moved here recently and worked in Broward County for a while as a police officer. Now, he wants to work as a detective. He scored high on the tests. Says he was an EMT for a few years."

"Really? Why the switch?"

"He said he was born to be a cop."

"When does he start?"

"This week. I'm waiting for some paperwork and he's moving into a new house."

"What's his name?"

"Mike Angel."

Elena's heart flip flopped in her chest. Was he an angel?

'*Yes*,' came from Lia. What were the chances of this happening again?

"Any more questions?" the captain asked.

"No, sir. I'll work on those reports now." She quickly left the office and headed to her desk. She sat with her elbows on the desk and her head in her hands. '*Now what? What is happening here? Lia, speak to me.*'

'*Mike Angel was an angel. He is human now and is married to a nurse. He trained under Pete as a Guardian Angel.*' Lia said.

She would wait and tell Pete about this later. There was nothing he could do now, anyway.

Elena sat and worked on her reports, making notes of things to do or look for as she went.

"There you are," Keith said. He stood before her at her desk.

"Hey, what's up?"

"I put some reports on Pete's desk about the perps you had been looking for. Did he share it with you?"

"He mentioned it, but I haven't seen the reports," she said.

"I'll get them. He's still on sick leave, right?"

"Yes. Did you hear what happened?"

"Yes, the captain filled me in. I'll be right back with that folder."

Within minutes, Keith returned with the promised folder. "If Pete is looking for this, tell him I gave it to you."

"Thanks, Keith, you're a life saver. This will help me with my reports." While skimming through the folder, she discovered that all the break-ins were done by the deceased from the warehouse incident. She finished writing up the reports with the proper information this time and took them to the captain.

"That was quick," the captain said.

"Now that the burglary cases are solved, I've still got some loose ends to tie up today and the possibility of a stake-out on Wednesday night, so I will work then instead of in the morning."

"What kind of back-up do you need?"

"Maybe Pete's team? They are familiar with part of the case."

"No can do. That's their night off. I'll find someone else to back you up. Besides, Pete and Jenkins are still out on sick leave. I expect Jenkins in this afternoon to work on reports. How's Pete's shoulder? Do you think he can shoot again? He'll have to qualify this month."

"Oh, yes, he will be able to qualify, but I'll let him fill you in. He has two appointments with doctors today."

"So, now that you've solved the burglary cases, you won't need that storefront downtown, will you?"

"I think the security company may be tied in with the drug dealers that Pete and his team were working on because the security company claimed all their installers were sick just after the recent incident at the warehouse. I don't think it's a coincidence that all the burglars were identified as the deceased at the same time the installers all got sick, do you?"

"You said it had something to do with the burglaries," the captain said.

"All the burglars were killed in the warehouse incident and that warehouse had drugs in it. I think it may be one organization running two different businesses. We haven't captured the main people yet, that's why I think Pete's team would be helpful. They were already working on the case."

"I'll think about it and get back with you on it. I just don't see how I can use that team on their night off, when I have other teams that can do the job."

"Yes, sir." Elena left and headed to her favorite sandwich shop downtown.

Alona and Teresa were busy with customers when she got inside. She stood in line and waited for her turn. It was good to see they were busy. That meant business was good. Of course, being the only sandwich shop in this neighborhood almost guaranteed that, didn't it?

Finally, it was her turn, and she ordered her favorite ham and Swiss wrap with water and chips. There was no one else behind her in line, so she started up a conversation.

"How are you both doing?"

"Oh, nice to see you again, Detective Cummings," Alona said.

"Tell her," Teresa said.

"Tell me what?" Elena asked.

"I need some help. Do you know any lawyers?" Alona asked.

"Why, yes, I do. I have two brothers-in-law who are

both lawyers." She rummaged through her purse and pulled out their cards. "Here. Call them. They are both good people and this one," she pointed to Rick's card, "was a cop and is now a lawyer, so he knows the ins and outs of both sides."

"Bless you, thank you," Alona said.

"Will you be all right?" Elena asked.

"I hope so. I don't want to leave and start over. I like it here."

"Why would you do that?"

"The warehouse...I defended myself, but I should have used the methods that Luke showed me. Instead, I reverted to my old ways."

Elena touched Alona's arm. "I know you defended yourself, Alona. If you need me for anything, call me." Elena pulled out her own card and handed it to Alona.

"Thank you," Alona said.

Elena took her sandwich to go, thinking she would eat in her pretend business. Once she passed the Martial Arts Studio, she decided to see if Luke was there.

Luke sat with her for a few minutes.

"She's having a hard time changing old ways and now she's dealing with the courts on the matter of defending herself," he said.

"Does she know you're an angel?"

"Not yet."

"Maybe it's time you took the training up a notch."

"What do you mean?"

"Whenever she reverts to her old ways, give it back to her so she can see what she's doing. Maybe that will force her to rethink how she reacts."

"If I do that, she will know I'm an angel."

"Is knowing so bad? I knew Pete was an angel when I

first worked with him. I think I'm still good. We get along great, except he was injured recently."

"Can he still heal himself?"

"Yes, as a matter of fact, he can still do many things except fight a demon."

"Which demon?"

"The one that had something to do with the burglaries on this street. I think he still has something to do with the security company that will be installing the security in my business next door. Will you be able to watch them for me on Wednesday night?"

"Yes. I'll have to work something out, but yes, I'll do it."

"Good. I'll either be staking out the place or driving around on patrol. I hope to have a backup as well."

"You know, you won't be able to stop the demon yourself?"

"Yes, I know. That's why I need your help. Pete is willing to help me, but he said only an angel can chain up a demon."

"He's right. You'll need to call on a legion of angels for Wednesday night. That's the only backup you'll really need."

"Thanks, Luke."

"Oh, one more thing," Luke said. He stood up and walked her to the door of his office.

"Yes?"

"You had some furniture delivered on Friday. I went ahead and let them in for you."

"Oh, my goodness! I forgot all about it. I had a family emergency and left town. How did you get inside?"

"I can become invisible. I went through the back door and opened the front door from the inside."

"Thank you so much. You know, Alona is worried about this court case?"

"Yes. I told her to speak to you about a lawyer. I knew you could help her."

Elena left and headed to her business. She unlocked the door and stood inside, glancing around the room. The thought that this would make a good detective's office flashed through her mind.

12

———

When Elena got home, there were two vehicles in the driveway. One was Pete's red truck, the other was a black Buick. Where had she seen that vehicle before? She parked behind Pete's truck.

Inside, she found Jenkins on the chair and Pete sitting on the sofa, enjoying a couple of beers. "Well, nothing like almost getting killed to cement a friendship," she said.

Both men raised their beers in salute to her statement. Between the sofa and chair sat a small cooler. She sat beside Pete on the sofa. Pete leaned over and pulled a beer out of the cooler, opened it, and handed it to her.

"Join us," Pete said.

"Don't mind if I do," she said.

"We are officially not sick anymore," Jenkins said. He slurred his words a little.

"I can attest to that," she said. She raised her beer and then took a sip. She glanced at both men. "So, what's the occasion?" she asked.

"The captain told me to come in to work today to do reports," Jenkins said.

"And?"

"I told him I had a mandatory doctor appointment with a psychiatrist, and I would not be in."

She felt something wasn't right and held her breath.

"The captain said, "You will be in this afternoon, or you're fired."

"No!" She let out her breath.

Jenkins smiled and raised his beer. "Yep, I'm fired," he said.

She glanced at Pete. He raised his brows.

"You, too?"

Pete smiled and nodded.

She jumped off the sofa. "He fired both of you, after you were almost killed?"

"Yep," Pete said.

Hmm. It sounded like they had been drinking for a while. She walked into the kitchen and noticed a half-empty case of beer sitting on the table. The case contained a dozen empty bottles. She glanced around the kitchen. Nothing was being cooked. She dialed the pizza delivery number and ordered two large pizzas. She returned to the living room.

"What did your other team members say when you told them?" she asked.

Pete pulled her arm toward him, and she sat down next to him once more. A drunk angel was not something she had been prepared to deal with.

"Heins and Struber now have to do the work of four people," Jenkins said. He spoke slower now and still slurred his words.

"What did the psychiatrist say?" she asked.

"He gave us a clean bill of sale," Pete said.

She blinked. "You mean a clean bill of health?"

"Yeah, that's it." Pete said.

"What about the other doctor, at the hospital?"

"Same," Pete said.

She put her beer down on the coffee table and held Pete's face in her hands.

"Hmm. You don't appear drunk." *'Pete are you coherent?'* she asked, telepathically.

'Yes, I'm coherent and I'm not drunk. It's just an act.'

She raised an eyebrow at that. Pete winked at her. She let go of his face. "Well, I ordered a couple of pizzas, so let's get some water in both of you." She stood and collected the empty beer bottles and headed for the kitchen. There, she added them to the case on the table. She poured two large glasses of ice water and brought them into the living room. She gave one glass to each of them. "Drink up, boys, if you want some pizza." She stood with her hands on her hips.

Jenkins gulped his down and then headed to the bathroom. She moved next to Pete on the sofa. "What happened?" she whispered.

"Just like Jenkins said, he was fired."

"What about you?"

"The captain called me after I saw my doctor and said the hospital called him and said there was nothing wrong with me."

"And?"

"He fired me for lying and saying I was shot."

"What?"

Jenkins came out of the bathroom. "I think I better head on home," he said.

Pete stood. "No, you're staying here for the night. We have a guest room." Pete turned him around and showed him where the room was.

The pizza delivery guy showed up. Elena took care of the pizza and had napkins and plates out for the three of them.

She heard Pete's phone ringing in the guest bedroom. When he came out, he had an announcement. "Heins and Struber will be joining us in a little bit."

"Really? I'm glad I ordered two large pizzas." She went back into the kitchen to grab a couple more plates and napkins.

As everyone settled into their seats with their pizza and drink, there was a knock at the door. Elena answered it. "Come on in, boys, we're having a party." She ushered Struber and Heins inside. "How about water or soda?" she asked.

Struber pointed to a beer bottle on the coffee table. "How about one of those?"

"Me, too," Heins said.

"Two beers, Pete," she said.

Pete reached into the small cooler and pulled out two more beers, handing them to Elena. She handed each man a beer. Then she went into the kitchen and retrieved a chair, since both men took up the remaining comfortable seats in the living room. She staked out a spot near Pete and close to the kitchen.

"I thought you two were working tonight," Pete said.

"We were until the captain put us both on leave without pay for lying on our reports," Heins said.

"Lying about what?" Pete asked.

"Lying about seeing you both get shot and applying first aid until the ambulance arrived," Struber said.

"What about the EMTs? Didn't they see the injuries? Elena asked.

"And the doctor who performed the surgery?" Jenkins asked.

"That's who I saw today," Pete said. "He was astonished there was no evidence of an injury. I explained that I believed all healing comes from God and I prayed for a healing. He didn't like that answer."

Elena took a swig of her beer. "I guess he won't like it when we don't pay for the surgery or hospital stay, either."

"I think we all need a lawyer," Jenkins said.

"We have two in the family," Pete said.

"That's right!" Elena stood and found her purse. She rummaged through it to find the business cards they gave her each time they got together. "Here you go," she said. She handed each of them two cards.

"Rick Johnson?" Struber said.

"Yes?" Elena stood watching for his reaction.

"I went to school with him. We both majored in criminal justice," Struber said.

After a few hours of commiserating, Struber drove Jenkins home in Jenkins' car, while being followed by Heins in Heins' car. The plan was Heins would drop off Struber at Struber's house after that.

Elena and Pete cleaned up the mess. Afterward, Pete headed to the bedroom and lay down on the bed. Elena came in the room and fell back onto the bed. "What a mess! Just because they can't handle the truth about your healing, they are calling everyone a liar." She glanced over at Pete. "How are you feeling about all of this?"

He rolled over on his side to face her. He reached his arm toward her and rested his hand on her stomach. "I'm a fast learner. I can do anything. But I really like this detective work. It suits me. It suits you." He drew small circles with his fingers on her belly. "I've been thinking, though, that Catalina had a great idea at the first dinner."

"Oh?" She knew exactly what he was talking about.

"Yes, about us starting our own detective agency."

She turned toward him, on her side. "I had the same thought just today."

The next day, she had to make some big decisions. If Pete and his team were all fired, the captain might take it out on her and fire her as well. She went over her savings with Pete. She had enough to cover the rent of the office in the downtown building, plus pay back the department for their expenses. She contacted the real estate agent and found out the check had not been cashed. She made an appointment with the agent to exchange her check for the department's check. She headed into town to meet with her, while Pete dealt with her brother-in-law.

She met the agent at her new business location.

"What type of business are you planning on having?" the agent asked.

"A detective agency. Private detectives to be exact."

"That sounds interesting. Contact me when you are set up and I'll hand out your cards to my clients."

"I definitely will. Thank you." Elena sat at the desk and began to make a list of things to do. She would go back to the station and get her contact list together. She needed business right away and had to get the word out. She would also need the help of people in the department. There were times when they had to drop a case because it took too long and took away the detectives from other jobs. Maybe she could get some officers to refer people to her when they were strapped for manpower or time? As far as she knew, she didn't have any enemies, so maybe they would cooperate.

She also made another list of names to use for the

agency. It would be just her and Pete. When she couldn't think anymore, she decided to go to the sandwich shop and visit with the girls.

The visit was short as the two women were busy with customers.

"I have an appointment with your brothers-in-law next week," Alona said.

"Good. That's a start. I'm sure they can help you."

"We've been hopping this week," Teresa said. "We had to put in an extra order for food, but it won't come in until tomorrow night."

"I'll take care of it, Teresa. It's not your fault we've been busy," Alona said.

Elena waved goodbye and headed back to her new office to eat her sandwich. She would have to order a desk for Pete and a file cabinet. She added those two things to her list. When she finished, she headed back to the station. She didn't want to go there, but something told her she had too. Everything was set for the stakeout tomorrow night.

She dreaded seeing the captain after what he did to the four detectives, to Pete! She figured her days were numbered anyway.

Once inside the station, someone approached her. "The captain has been looking for you. He wants you in his office the minute you get here," she said.

Elena rolled her eyes. She really didn't want to see him. She knocked on his door.

"Come in!"

When she stepped inside, there was an officer standing there, speaking to the captain.

"Oh, sorry, sir. I'll come back when you aren't busy," she said. She backed out of the room.

"Romero, get in here!"

She stepped back inside. "It's Cummings, sir. Elena Romero Cummings."

The officer turned toward her and offered his hand. He had a dazzling smile and a dimple on his left check. He was quite handsome.

"Mike Angel. Nice to meet you, Detective Cummings."

"Oh, likewise." His hand was warm and his eyes friendly.

"How long have you known Cummings was lying about his injury?" the captain asked.

"He wasn't lying, sir. I visited him in the hospital. I talked to the surgeon. I brought my husband home."

"There's no way someone can heal that fast and not have a mark on him," the captain said.

"I beg to differ, sir." Mike said. He glanced at the captain, then Elena.

"I have healed many people in my short time as an EMT. It's a miracle, that's what it is. There is no explanation necessary unless you are an unbeliever. People can actually heal themselves."

"Are you calling me an unbeliever?" the captain asked. He stood up and leaned on his desk.

"Do you believe in God?" Mike asked.

"Of course, I do!"

"Do you believe in the power of faith? In miracles?"

"That's different," the captain said. He sat down.

"It's no different. If you have faith, all things are possible," Mike said.

"Amen!" Elena added. She turned to Mike. "He just fired four detectives for using their faith and called them all liars," she said.

Mike slowly shook his head. "I thought you were short-handed in this department, that's why I applied and made the move from Pensacola to here." He turned toward Elena.

"I may have to rethink working for this department," he said.

She held up a finger, motioning him to wait. She handed the check to the captain. "Here's the money I got from the department for the office space downtown. "I may rethink working here as well." She turned and walked out the door with Mike.

At her desk, she hurriedly gathered the few things that actually belonged to her and headed outside. "Well, I think you and my husband, Pete, would have hit it off just fine."

"Pete?" He stopped walking and touched her shoulder. "Can you picture him for me?"

"Sure." She closed her eyes and thought of Pete, then opened her eyes when she realized the truth. "You're an angel?"

"Was. And so was Pete, wasn't he?"

"He said he trained someone named Mike to be a Guardian Angel."

"Let's go see Pete."

Elena gave her address to Mike and then headed home. He followed behind her in his black truck, pulling in behind her in the driveway.

When she got inside, she called out. "Pete, we have company." She heard something in the kitchen and headed there. Pete was at the stove, wearing an apron and stirring something on the stove. "Hello, Pete!"

He turned and stared at their guest. "Mike?"

"Yeah, it's me. In the flesh."

Pete moved toward him and gave him a big hug. "What are you doing here in Miami?"

"I thought I was going to become a detective and work with your wife, but now, I don't know."

"What do you mean?" Pete asked.

Mike turned toward Elena and back to Pete. "Elena and I had a discussion with the captain. It seems he doesn't believe in miracles or healings."

"Sad, isn't it?"

"Yes. More disturbing than anything. Maria and I just moved here from Pensacola. We're expecting our first child."

"Congratulations!" Elena said. She patted his arm. "Can I get you anything to drink?"

"Water would be fine," Mike said.

Elena busied herself with that task while the two men talked. After handing Mike his drink, she took over the cooking so they could visit.

About an hour later, Mike got ready to leave.

"Elena and I are doing a stakeout tomorrow night on a business downtown. She's following up on a security company that may be involved in some illegal activities."

"You're doing this alone? Without backup?"

"Well, three detectives who were fired along with me, as well as an angel," Pete said.

"An angel?"

"Yes. I think there's a demon involved with this company."

"A demon, huh? Any idea which one?"

"No, but maybe Luke knows. We'll find out one way or another."

"Count me in. I don't know how much help I can offer, but we can distract him for the angel to deal with him," Mike said.

"Absolutely."

The two exchanged phone numbers and Mike left.

Pete walked up behind Elena and hugged her. "I had a nice, long conversation with Rick and Juan today. They said we all have a good case."

"Of course, you do. What the captain did was wrong."

"There's too much evidence to prove we were both injured."

"So, what did they say?"

"They want the case. Rick said he worked under the captain years ago. Juan said your dad knew the captain when they worked together."

"Yes, I forgot about that." She turned around to face him. "Supper's ready."

Together, they set the food on the bar and sat down to eat. After giving thanks for their food, Pete froze.

"What is it?" Elena asked.

"Something's not right."

"What? Is it the food?"

"No. It's this situation. Everything that's happening right now."

She waited for the punch line. She was missing something. "The firing of you four?"

"That and the sudden appearance of Mike. What name is he using?"

"He didn't tell you?"

"No. In heaven, we only have one name. When I appeared in the flesh, I had to have two names, so Cummings was given to me. Mike was always just Mike."

"His last name is Angel."

Pete laughed. "That figures."

"But you have doubts about everything. What is it that's making you feel that way?" Elena asked.

"The behavior of the captain. Not believing in miracles. The fact that he fired four good detectives. Mike's sudden appearance. I think God is setting something in motion."

"Something good, I hope."

"Or maybe he's preparing us for something bad."

Elena reached for Pete's hand. "Let's pray for a legion of angels to surround us and fight this demon, in Jesus' name."

"Amen."

Later in the evening, while Pete and Elena snuggled together, he whispered in her ear. "There's something I didn't tell you about Mike."

"There's a lot you didn't tell me about Mike," she said.

"Well, he was once human."

"Oh?"

"He was killed in the line of duty."

"That's sad."

"Yes, by his partner."

She turned in his arms. "Murdered?"

"Yes."

"How tragic."

"He was murdered twice by the same man."

"How did that even happen?"

"The first time he died, I trained him to be a Guardian. When he returned to Earth, his person was Maria. What Mike didn't know was Maria was the reincarnation of his dead wife, who was also murdered by his ex-partner just after giving birth to their son, whom Mike never knew about."

"You mean his partner killed his pregnant wife?"

"No. He waited until she returned home with the baby. She went into labor when she learned Mike had been killed and was rushed to the hospital. Mike's partner thought she knew something about what he was up to and had her killed by his thugs."

Elena sat up. "I hope they were all punished!"

"His partner died that night of a heart-attack and his spirit was taken to hell. He shot Mike the second time, while he was in the flesh, protecting Maria. God gave Mike another chance, so this baby is the spirit of the baby they had lost before."

"Does Mike know all this?"

"Probably not. It's hard to remember the spirit world once you are in the flesh and vice versa."

"How did you know all this?"

"I've always been an angel. When I crossed over, I was able to keep my memories."

"So, reincarnation is real?"

"Yes. Haven't you ever met someone and felt as if you knew them before?"

"I think so, yes."

"And some families stay together, reincarnating over and over in the same family units."

"That's fascinating."

"Heaven is a fascinating place."

13

———

Late afternoon, Elena and Pete drove downtown in her Mustang. They parked in the nearby parking garage and made frequent trips around the neighborhoods, watching for anything suspicious. There was no chatter on the radio, but she didn't know if the captain had set up a backup team for her.

Pete, on the other hand, got his crew to set up in different places to wait. They all had their own portable radios, since they had turned in their equipment.

Elena contacted Luke telepathically. *'Is everything set on your end, Luke?'*

'Yes, I'm in my studio next door, waiting.'

Once darkness settled over the area, Elena pulled to a stop along the street, down from the office in question, and waited. She had been keyed up all day. Pete reached over and held her hand. "Got your armor on?"

"No! I forgot it."

"Let's do this together," he said. He recited the passage from Ephesians, while they both put on their armor of God. Then, he squeezed her hand once more.

A van pulled up outside her office. She and Pete watched four men get out and unload some equipment. She had been told to leave the door unlocked, so she did. They watched the men move the equipment inside.

"I don't recognize any of them," Pete said, looking through binoculars. He handed them to Elena.

"I don't either. From here, it's too hard to identify any of them anyway." Something caught her eye. She raised the glasses once again. "It looks like they're wearing rubber gloves. Why would they do that?"

"That's a good question. We only arrested the management of those businesses involved in distributing those stuffed bears," Pete said.

"That leaves the people who actually stuffed the bears," Elena said.

Pete's phone vibrated. "Yes, go ahead," he said.

"I see something going on in the back of the alley," Jenkins said. "It looks like they are putting up some small cameras."

She glanced at Pete. "Why would they do that?"

"It looks like they are putting them in strategic places on other businesses," Jenkins said.

Elena glanced toward Pete and noticed a light on in another shop. Through the dimness, she saw someone moving around. She studied the figure and realized it was Alona, stocking her shop. She motioned to Pete, and he watched Alona as well, until another figure appeared out of nowhere. A man stood in the front part of the store walking toward Alona.

"What in the world?" Elena said.

"That is from the underworld," Pete said. He opened the car door while dialing Struber. "We got someone inside the sandwich shop that shouldn't be there," he said.

Elena got out of her side of the car. *'Luke, Alona has company,'* she sent telepathically.

Luke arrived before she and Pete could get to the door. He moved toward the door then headed toward Alona. When Elena got to the door, Luke was gone.

Alona glanced up and realized she had company.

"Who are you?" she asked the man who stood between Alona and her rescuers.

"Raum. I've come to ask your help, Noura Hashim. It's taken me a couple thousand years to find you."

"Whatever you're selling, I'm not interested," she said.

Elena and Pete moved quietly behind the man.

"Oh, I know you're there, officers. There's no need to worry. I'm not interfering with anything."

With the element of surprise gone, there wasn't much they could do, but Elena had her weapon ready in her shoulder holster.

"You are trespassing. Now leave or I will have them arrest you," Alona said.

"There isn't anything they can do to me, Noura. You should know that."

"You can leave. I don't want anything to do with you," she said.

"You haven't let me explain what I want with you, Noura," Raum said.

"Quit calling me Noura. I know what you are here for and you can't have it."

"Well, if I can't have your cooperation and help, I'll just take their souls."

Pete blinked and everyone was wearing a suit of God's Armor. Mike came out of the back of the shop, also wearing God's Armor.

"Oh, so you brought reinforcements?" Raum glanced

around. In a single movement, Raum shot out fire darts at all of them, but they fell away from the armor.

"You know why I've been searching for you all these years, don't you?"

"No! And I don't want to know," Alona said.

"You are one of us."

"No, I'm not. I serve the Lord God, All Mighty. I will never serve your master!" She shouted and pointed at him.

Suddenly, Elena saw the legion of angels she had prayed for. They were everywhere, crowding into the small shop. Along the ceiling and every wall, and they all wore the armor of God. They gave off a bright, golden light.

"Oh, but you will. I insist."

Raum shot huge, powerful fire darts at Alona, over and over. Her shield grew large and took the blows, but the force of his darts pushed her back against the wall. Watching the darts pummel her shield, made Elena feel helpless, until some of the angels deflected the darts back at Raum. Alona could only defend herself against this demon. The legion of angels moved to surround Raum, protecting Alona and the others from Raum's fire darts.

Elena wanted to do more. She moved to grab a chair, but one hand held the sword and the other, the shield.

'Don't let your guard down, Elena. Use your sword,' Pete spoke to her telepathically.

Pete moved closer to Raum from behind, while Mike moved in from the front. Both men took a charging stance against Raum, while Raum continued his forceful shots at Alona. Raum simultaneously shot fire darts at Mike and Pete with the other hand. Elena moved in quickly and stabbed Raum in the back with the sword of truth, paralyzing him momentarily.

'Great move, babe!' Pete spoke telepathically. *'Keep it up.'*

Mike and Pete continued their assaults, distracting Raum. Elena pulled her sword free and stabbed Raum again in a different place. Each time, he froze momentarily, giving everyone a breather. But he was relentless on Alona, never letting up on her assaults. The legion of angels kept deflecting his darts, protecting her.

Suddenly, Luke appeared with spiritual chains and tossed them around Raum in one swift motion. Luke floated up with Raum under his control, a sword at Raum's throat. Raum's arms were constrained against his sides. In a moment, they were gone, followed by the legion of angels. All the swords and shields disappeared.

Elena ran to Alona, who had collapsed on the floor. "Are you all right?"

Alona struggled to prop herself up. "Thank you," she said.

Elena helped her up off the floor. Pete and Mike continued their vigilance in her shop.

"Sometimes demons have underlings that tag along," Pete said.

Elena had her arm around Alona, supporting her, while they walked to a stool.

"He drained me," Alona said. "I've never felt this weak before."

"Have you ever fought a demon before?" Elena asked.

"No."

"Me neither. I think we did well for our first time," Elena said. "You were fantastic, the way you held up under fire. I don't think I could have done that."

"Luke is an angel," Alona said.

"Yes, he told me."

"How long have you known?"

"A little before you did," Elena said. "He tried to protect you for as long as he could."

"Protect me from what? Raum?"

"I think so. He didn't want you hurt."

"I protected myself."

"Yes, but only an angel can chain up an evil spirit. We did this as a team. We worked well together."

"I think we're safe for now," Pete said.

"What gifts do you have?" Mike asked Alona.

"I have my strength and I can grow to sixteen feet. Luke was teaching me martial arts," Alona said.

"That's a good skill to have. Keep up the work," Mike said.

Elena heard a scraping sound in the ceiling. "What's that?"

Everyone stopped to listen. Alona stretched to ceiling height and pushed up on a tile. There was a cable being pushed through the ceiling. Alona grabbed the cable and pulled it into the shop. "What is this?" she asked.

"They are supposed to be installing security cameras in my office, several shops down," Elena said.

Pete rushed to the front door and headed outside, toward Elena's office.

"Stay here," Mike said. He rushed out the back door.

Elena made a motion with her finger to be quiet. She put her arm around Alona's shoulder. Alona held the cable in her hand.

A police unit drove by Alona's shop, without the siren. After twenty minutes, Pete spoke to her telepathically. *'Everything's okay, babe. We arrested the security people. I'll be back soon.'*

"What's going on?" Alona asked. She appeared to have regained her strength.

Elena explained what her original plan was, but after Alona dispatched the security team, another team had to be put together. And because she wanted to know who was involved in this new team and why they were so secretive about the installation.

When she finished explaining, Luke appeared.

"Luke?" Alona went to him, and they embraced.

"We have a lot of things to catch up on," he said.

"Yes, we do."

Luke turned to Elena. "Your police backup came through. Raum had your captain under his control. You'll find things will be somewhat normal after this."

"Where are Pete and Mike?"

"They are assisting the police. What you decide to do after tonight is up to you. Just know that Alona and I will be glad to assist you whenever the need arises."

"Thank you, Luke."

Luke snapped his fingers and everything in the shop went back to normal. The food had been put away and all the furniture had been straightened back up. "If you leave now, I can lock up," Luke said.

Elena took her cue and left out the front door. She glanced through the window and saw Luke and Alona embracing and kissing. Then, poof, they were gone. She smiled and headed for all the action near her new office.

Elena found Pete and Mike outside the office, talking to an officer and several other men. When she got closer, she realized it was Pete's team of Jenkins, Heins, and Struber speaking to another officer she didn't know. One patrol vehicle had just left with two prisoners. A tow truck pulled away, hauling the security company's van.

An officer sat in the front seat with two prisoners in the back as she glanced inside the vehicle. The officer Pete's team had been talking to climbed inside his vehicle and left.

Pete put his arm around her. "We did good tonight," he said.

"Oh? Other than defeat a demon?"

"Yes, we captured some hardened drug dealers."

"And how do you know this?"

"Their rap sheets," Jenkins said. He handed her several sheets of paper.

"How did you get these so quick?"

"I did some research on that warehouse where the drugs were distributed from. These four showed up in several searches as wanted men."

"Now all we have to do is find out who stuffed and sewed those bears," Heins said.

"Good deal. Any leads?" Elena asked.

"Not yet, but maybe we can get one of these four to sing since we have all the big players," Struber said.

"Well, it was nice meeting the three of you," Mike said. "But I have a wife and dinner waiting for me at home."

"Thank you, Mike, for all your help," Elena touched his arm.

"No problem. Call me any time," Mike said. He left and headed to his vehicle out back. The three men from Pete's team drifted back to their vehicles. Elena and Pete stepped inside her office.

"Let's clean this up tomorrow," she said. Pete had his hands on his hips, glancing around.

"I'll lock up the back," he said.

She waited by the front door for Pete. When he returned, he smiled at her. "I've got it," he said.

"You've got what?" They stepped out onto the sidewalk as she locked the front door.

"Guardian Investigations," he said.

She studied his face. "I like that. Guardian Investigations it is. And if we need backup, Luke and Alona will be there for us," she said.

"And if we need help from the local police department, we've got four detectives who will be available to help us out," Pete said.

She put her arm through Pete's as they headed to her Mustang. She drove home as Pete sat back in the passenger seat.

"What are you thinking?" she asked.

"Just wondering what tomorrow will bring."

"A new start for both of us," she said.

The next morning, while they cuddled in bed, Elena's phone rang.

"Just let it go to voicemail," Pete said. He kissed her behind her ear. She held her breath until it stopped ringing. When the kisses became steamy, the phone rang again.

"This isn't going to work," she said. She reached for her phone. It was the captain. "Hello?"

"Romero, I owe you and Cummings an apology," he said.

"It's Cummings, sir," she said.

"That's what I said."

"You called me Romero. My name is Cummings, the same as Pete. Why do you owe us an apology?" She hit the speaker on her phone.

"I do believe in God, and I do believe in miracles. I apologize for my, uh, error in judgement."

"I forgive you, captain," she said. Pete leaned in. "I forgive you, too, captain."

"I need you both back at work as soon as possible."

"Well, captain, there's been a change in plans," she said.

"Oh?"

"Yes, sir. Pete and I are starting our own detective agency. And Mike Angel will make a great addition to Jenkins' team, don't you think?"

"What?"

"You have re-hired Jenkins, Struber, and Heins, haven't you?"

"Uh, yes, I did. Mike Angel, huh? I'll consider that. Yes, that's a good idea."

After a leisurely breakfast, the two headed downtown to the new office. Elena had her computer with her as they drove in Pete's truck. It only took a couple hours, but they managed to pull all the cables the security team stuffed into their ceiling. They put things back in order and arranged the office so it looked inviting. While Elena made lists of things she needed, Pete went out back and removed the cameras the security team put up outside. When he returned, she handed him the list.

"Take a look at this list and see if I'm missing anything?" she said.

"How about a sign for our front window, so people know who we are and what we do?"

"Excellent idea." She called the real estate agent who sold her the lease and inquired if she knew someone who did the signs in this building. She took down the name and number and then made a call. "They will be here tomorrow," she said. Pete sat on the edge of the desk.

"We should get some furniture in here, so our clients won't have to sit on the desk," Pete said.

"Another excellent idea. Let's lock up and go shopping."

There was a furniture store not far from the office, so they headed to it. Elena picked out two comfy chairs, which Pete tested, a small table, another desk and chair for a receptionist, and some bathroom items. They arranged for them to be delivered the next day. The two continued with the other things on the list, which took them to another area of town. By the time they got everything on the list, it was quitting time.

While Pete drove home, Elena doodled on a pad of paper. "We need some business cards printed," she said.

After fixing dinner together, Pete sat with Elena on the sofa and they designed their business cards. She had her laptop with her and almost put in the order, until she realized they needed a phone number. "We'll have to finish this tomorrow after I get a phone number for our business. We can always add our cell phones to it, but we need someone here to take the calls and run errands."

"What else do we need?" Pete asked.

"We need business. Lots of business and we have to figure out what to charge." They went over the cost of the office space, the furnishings and equipment, the electric, and any other costs they could possibly come up with. Then, they figured out what they made per hour and how much they would need to cover their costs. It took the rest of the night to finalize their costs and projections. But now they had a plan.

On the way to their new business the next morning, Elena began a list of businesses she would call to get the word out. Once they got there, she made a call to get a phone line put in.

Then she started making calls to drum up business. She started with insurance companies. There were a lot, so it took a big part of the morning. Before she could finish, the furniture arrived and so did the sign painter.

She took care of the furniture people, while Pete worked with the sign painter. Once the furniture people left, she headed down to the sandwich shop to pick up a couple sandwiches for her and Pete. Pete remained behind with the sign painter.

When she returned, the phone company was installing their new phone. Since she had already gotten the new phone number, the sign painter had it painted on the door. He painted a really nice sign across the large window in the front of the office.

Elena had time to order her business cards now that everything else was taken care of. She had just finished her online order when a woman rushed into the office. Pete, sitting at the reception desk, stood.

"Can we help you?" he asked.

Elena glanced up from her computer. And so, it began.

NEPHILIM

Her name, Noura Hashim, means light destroys evil. And that's what she had done for the last two thousand years. But the times had changed and she had to adjust. When her secret got out, she had to change her name and move to another town, another state, another country, and finally another continent. Her crusade was to stop bullies and fight evil wherever she could. It used to be easy, but with the changing attitudes and times, it was more difficult to deal with the criminals of each town.

She found herself in Miami. It was the perfect mixture of different races and cultures and she blended in well. She settled down there and changed her name to Alona Gabriel. She bought a small shop and set up business in the downtown area.

With the Miami-Dade Police Department, she felt she was finally able to live a normal life and not get involved in fighting crime. It took her a little time to get the word out that she was open for business. Working hard, she was able to make a living. She bought a townhouse and felt like she belonged here. Soon, her business grew and she hired a young woman to help her. Everything seemed perfect until one day, a demon walked into her shop. She smelled his evil scent the minute he walked in her door. He approached the counter.

"Are you the manager?" he asked.

"Yes. How can I help you?" She really wanted to help him out of her store.

"I'm in the security business and I see you don't have any security systems in place."

"I have my own security system, thank you."

"Really? And what is that?" He placed his hands on her counter. He held a business card in his fingers.

"I don't want to discuss it. Now, if you aren't buying a sandwich, I suggest you leave."

"Very well. I'll leave my card in case you change your mind." He set the card down in front of her.

She glared at him with no expression on her face. Then she watched him slowly leave.

Teresa came up behind her. "Who was that? He was cute. Did you get his number?"

"He was a demon. You don't want to have anything to do with him. Trust me."

Teresa reached for the card.

"Don't touch that!" she shouted.

"What?"

She grabbed a napkin and scooped up the card. She carried it outside to the back trash cans. When she returned, she washed her hands in very hot water and lots of soap.

"What was that about?"

She picked up the sanitizer and sprayed the counter with it. Then she wiped it down with several paper towels. "It's hard to get a demon scent out of anything," she said.

She went back outside with the dirty paper towels and tossed them in the trash receptacle.

"He was just a guy. A very good-looking guy at that. How can you say he was a demon? Did you know him?" Teresa asked.

"No. I can smell a demon. It's a very foul odor. Can't you smell it?"

"No. Are you talking about demons like in Satan and the devils that followed him?"

"Yes. If that's what you want to call him. He was a demon, a devil, an evil spirit in a human form."

"How do you know all this? I mean, he looked like a normal person. He was perfect."

"Yes. Looks can be so deceiving, can't they?"

Teresa looked puzzled.

"There's something about me you don't know." Should she tell her the truth? Would Teresa be able to handle the truth?

"Like what?"

"There's only a few of us who can sense demons or evil spirits. It takes practice, though."

"Yeah, right."

"Have you ever had the feeling that something feels bad, or dangerous? Or have you ever had the feeling like you need to get away from a certain place?"

"Yes. A time or two, but not many."

"Pay attention to that feeling. If you have it again, run. Run as fast as you can. And if you ever see that guy again, run like Satan is chasing you. Got it?"

"Sure, sure."

The doorbell chimed as a customer came inside. She glanced at her watch. 11:30 am. Lunch has started. She would let Teresa make the sandwiches until it started hopping, then she would step in and help out. She got here early every day to prep her little kitchen. She had an order coming in today and would handle that herself, while Teresa made the sandwiches. Teresa was a good worker. She would eventually teach her everything so she could take time off. Then again, maybe she would just close the shop for a week and they would both be off. It had been a long time since she had a vacation. Being downtown, she was able to be closed on the weekends because no one came into the shop on the weekends. This was the perfect little business, and she enjoyed it.

During the day, most of her customers were regulars. She and Teresa chatted with them while making their sandwiches. She took turns with Teresa and let her ring up for a while, while she made the sandwiches.

Finally, it was about three in the afternoon when the food truck came in. Teresa worked the shop, while she checked the items and inventoried everything and put the food away. By the time she finished, it was almost 4:00 pm. Closing time was 6:00 pm. She rejoined Teresa in the shop. Teresa was busy making sandwiches for a pickup.

"How's it going?" she asked.

"We have a couple pickup orders if you want to help me," Teresa said.

"Sure. What've you got?"

Teresa handed her the written order. "I'm finishing up this one."

Before she finished her order, a new customer came in. She did a double take because the guy looked nice. He was taller than her 6' frame with blondish-brown hair and brown eyes. Hmm. Teresa beat her to him.

"Hello, this your first time here?"

"Does it show?" he asked.

"Well, I haven't seen you in here before, so yes, it does. What'll you have?"

"Hmm, I'll have the number three and a drink."

"Sure thing." Teresa turned toward her.

"I got it, Teresa. You can ring it up."

She hurriedly made the Italian salami, ham, and pepperoni sandwich while Teresa talked to him. When she finished, she handed it to him and smiled. She couldn't help it. But she sensed something different about him. Was he a spiritual being? She didn't feel anything negative around him.

"I'll get your drink," Teresa said. She moved past her to get the drink.

"Hi," he said.

"Hi. I'm Alona and I own this shop." She reached her hand out to shake his. His grip was firm, and his hand felt warm and strong.

"Nice to meet you, Alona. I'm Luke. I work down the street at the Martial Arts Academy. Hope you'll stop by some time and check us out."

"I'd love to, thanks."

"Here's your drink." Teresa handed him the drink. "Come back and see us," she said.

"Oh, yes. I'll be back. Thank you, ladies."

She and Teresa watched him walk out.

"Now that's a fine-looking man," she said.

"Yes, he is. Did you get any bad vibes about him?" Teresa asked.

"No, but I did get some vibes."

Teresa stared at her. "What kind of vibes?"

"You know we're all spiritual beings, right?"

"Hmm. I never thought about it."

"Yes. We are all spiritual beings in a human body. He just seems more spiritual than normal."

"Is that good?" Teresa asked.

"If it's what I think it is, it is very good."

Alona closed up her sandwich shop about six o'clock and headed to the parking garage with Teresa. It had been a long day, but her shop took in a lot of money, and for that, she was grateful.

She had time to count out the drawer and put the cash into a bank bag she tucked into her purse.

"We did a lot of business this week, didn't we?" Teresa asked.

"Yes. I think it's because of the construction going on down the street." Suddenly, she sensed something was not right and stopped walking. She grabbed Teresa's arm to stop her and motioned with her finger against her lip to be quiet.

Teresa's eyes grew wide, but she remained silent.

A man appeared from behind a column. His hand was in his vest pocket. He pulled out his hand and held a gun, pointed at the two of them.

"Leave us alone," Alona said.

"I don't think so. What you got in that purse?" he asked.

"None of your business," Alona said. She clutched the purse close to her.

"I'll take your wallets. Both of you," he said.

"No, you won't," Alona said. She glanced at Teresa, who had reached in her purse. "Don't give him anything!" she said.

"He's got a gun," Teresa whispered.

"He's just a bully," she said.

"I'm not a bully, bitch. I just want your money. Hand it over or you both die." he said.

"Come and get it," she said.

He rushed toward Alona, but she was quicker. She grabbed his throat as he reached for hers, but she grew to over sixteen feet tall. She held his neck with her fingers, while he thrashed and kicked. He dropped his gun while clawing at her hand with both of his hands to free himself.

"Is this what you were planning on doing to me?" she asked.

He grew limp in her hand. She tossed him aside like a rag doll, then shrunk to her normal six-foot size.

Teresa stood staring at her. "What are you?"

She took Teresa's arm and turned her to face her. She snapped her fingers in Teresa's face. "Everything you've just seen, you will forget." Then she snapped her fingers again.

"My car is over there," Teresa pointed.

"I'll walk you to your car," she said.

"Thanks Alona." She opened her car door and climbed inside. "See you tomorrow."

"Tomorrow," she repeated. She headed toward her own car. The city wasn't as safe as she thought it was. Would she have to deal with this again? This was the first time it got violent in a long time. Usually, growing to sixteen feet was all she had to do, and they would run off. But this guy meant to harm them. She could feel the evil surrounding him. He even had the scent of a demon on him. It wasn't strong, but it was there all the same.

She climbed into her car and checked her surroundings before backing out. She didn't give the scumbag another thought as she drove home. She did go over, in her mind, the new customers she had today. Most of her customers worked in the near-by buildings. A few came from the construction site down the street. But today, she had a demon stop in the store, and an angel. Were these two entities the ones who had been tracking her the past two thousand years? Would she have to change her name again and move to another continent? She was tired of moving. She wanted to settle down in one place and live a normal life. Was that too much to ask, Lord?

Earlier, she remembered that feeling of foreboding she got, just before the demon showed up. In the past, it would make her paranoid. She ended up moving and changing her ID. Times were different now. Changing an ID and Social Security number was too difficult. Now she had a business to run and that made all the difference. She had settled down in the Miami area because so many people with different nationalities passed through here. She would be able to use all the languages she'd learned over the years.

Finally, she pulled into her subdivision which was made up of townhouse complexes. Her parking lot had a few cars in it already. It was dinner time, so there would be more people home in the next hour or so. She pulled into her spot and exited her car. Before she unlocked her door, she noticed a blondish-brown colored dog in the parking lot. They allowed pets here, but she never had one. She hated good-byes and since pets didn't live as long as people, she never got one. This one had beautiful hair coloring. There was something familiar about it, but she couldn't put her finger on it.

The dog moved toward her.

"Hello boy. Where do you belong?"

The dog sat and looked at her as if he understood what she asked. She reached a hand toward the dog, to let him sniff her. "Can I check your collar?" After he sniffed her, she petted him and realized he didn't have a collar. "I guess you don't have any people, do you?"

The dog cocked his head to the side. "Yeah, me neither."

She went to her neighbor's door on one side and knocked.

"Hello, Mrs. Turner. Do you know whose dog this is?" She pointed to the blondish-brown dog beside her.

"No. I sure don't. I haven't seen him around before. Why don't you try Mr. Johnson. He's home all day. Maybe he knows."

"Sure, thanks." She went to the door on the other side and knocked.

When she asked the same question, Mr. Johnson said, "No. I haven't seen him before. The only ones who have a dog is in the complex across from us. But their dog is a smaller breed."

"Thanks Mr. Johnson." She glanced at the patient dog beside her. "Well, would you like to have dinner with me?"

The dog stood and nodded. "In that case, follow me," she said. She walked toward her door and gestured for him to come in and he did.

She turned on her lights and set her purse down on a table near the entrance and locked the front door. The dog followed her into the kitchen.

She pulled containers of leftovers out of the fridge. "I have a lot to choose from tonight, so you're in luck."

After putting the food in microwaveable dishes, she heated them up. While they cooked, she pulled out a bowl and filled it with water. She set it down on the kitchen floor and the dog lapped up the water. Then she served him one dish of food and she took the other. She sat at the bar and gave thanks before she ate her meal. She watched the dog eat all the food.

"It looks like you enjoyed that." She put both dishes in the dishwasher and cleaned up the mess in the kitchen. "Let's see what's going on in the world." She walked into the living room, flipping on the tv, and sat on the couch. The dog followed her into the room and sat beside her on the floor.

She petted the dog while the world news was on. "You're pretty clean for a stray dog. What's your name, boy?"

The name Matthias came to her mind. "Is your name Matthias?" The dog wagged his tail and sat up straighter.

This was a first for her. Had he actually spoke to her? Did he understand what she was saying? "Well, Matthias, it's nice to meet you." She reached her hand out and Matthias put his paw into her hand, and she shook it. "Something tells me you're special."

Matthias barked.

"I take that as a yes." She watched Matthias walk to the door and sit. She got up and let him out, walking outside with him. She watched him do his thing. She would have to buy him a collar and leash if she kept him. The small dog park was down the street between two of the complexes. He came back quickly and they both went inside.

The local news was on when she sat back down on the sofa.

"This just in," the news reporter announced. "A body was found late this afternoon in a downtown Miami parking garage. The police are investigating the crime at this hour. We'll have more as it develops."

Her heart skipped a beat. The scene showed the parking garage where she and Teresa were accosted. She sat forward in her seat. A body lay covered in a body bag and crime scene tape was all over the place.

"Oh no!" Her heart pounded. She didn't think about the aftermath of what she had done.

The phone rang moments later, and she jumped.

"Hi Teresa. What's up?"

"Did you just see the news? That was our parking garage. Oh my God, Alona. We were there this afternoon. That could have been us."

"Well, just be thankful it wasn't us. I'm sure they will have security after this."

"I hope so."

"Don't give it another thought. Otherwise, you won't get any sleep. The police will do their job, and everything will be fine."

"Maybe we should start carrying guns," Teresa said.

"They are too heavy to put in my purse. I'll take my chances without one." She hoped Teresa would drop the subject. At least she didn't remember anything, and that was good. "I'll see you tomorrow, Teresa. Have a good night."

The reporter didn't mention cameras, so that was good. She went over the events in her mind. What could she have done differently? The man would have killed both of them. She had all the earnings from the store with her and she wasn't about to let some thug take it. She got up and retrieved her purse then returned to the sofa. She took the bank bag out of it and recounted the bills once more. Then she made out the deposit slip. First thing in the morning, she would make a deposit so she could pay each of them for their work this week.

"Well, Matthias, tomorrow I have a deposit to make before heading to work. I hope you have a strong bladder. I'll be gone all day." She leaned over and petted his head. He cocked his head, so she stroked his neck. He seemed to enjoy that, so she continued for a while. "If you decide to stay, I'll have to buy you a leash and some toys." She should probably have him checked by a vet. Maybe she should put an ad in the paper saying she found the dog. While she petted him, she thought of the new customer who came into her shop late in the day. "I met a guy today, Matthias. He was pretty hot. Hopefully, I'll see him again. Your hair color reminds me of him." She got the feeling that after tonight, her life would not be the same.

ABOUT THE AUTHOR

To keep up to date on the Ester's book releases, and to get the FREE "Vaedra Chronicles" companion book, please join Ester's Readers Group at:

www.esterlopez.com
Follow Ester's Blogs at:
www.esterlopez.com
www.authorblogspot.esterlopez.com
Follow Ester on:
www.facebook.com/EsterLopezAuthor
or on Twitter at:
www.twitter.com/esterlopez1
And if you like the story, please leave an honest review at your favorite bookseller
You can also join Ester's Group Page on Facebook at Virtual Book Signing & Takeover Group

ALSO BY ESTER LÓPEZ

The Angel Chronicles Series

The Quest

Between Heaven and Earth

Golden Idols

Bailey's Irish Dream

The Vaedra Chronicles Series

Genesis Saga

The Abduction

Revenge

Betrayed

Aftermath

Battle For Earth

Children's Books

The Adventures of Charlie and Ellie

Little Horses

Across The Big Ocean